Pra
At the

'I recommend it to everyone.'

Arthur Calder-Marshall

'A remarkable first novel.'

Evening Standard

'A laconic, merciless, appallingly accurate description
of life in an old people's home... It is so well done
that it is often not bearable.'

Spectator

'It extends human sympathy beyond the point
where it normally comes to a stop.'

Observer

'*At the Jerusalem*, Paul Bailey's first novel, would be
remarkable as the work of a writer over middle age;
from so young a man it is astounding in its empathy.'

Financial Times

'It would be difficult to praise this novel too highly.'

Daily Telegraph

'A display of pure style... A high-wire act, with not a sound
or a piece of dialogue left unchiseled, not a false note.'

Colm Tóibín

At the Jerusalem

At the Jerusalem

Paul Bailey

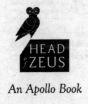

An Apollo Book

First published in 1967 by Jonathan Cape

This edition published in the United Kingdom in 2019 by Apollo,
an imprint of Head of Zeus Ltd
This Apollo paperback edition first published in the United Kingdom
in 2020 by Head of Zeus Ltd

1 3 5 7 9 10 8 6 4 2

A CIP catalogue record for this book is available
from the British Library.

ISBN (PB): 9781789545715
ISBN (E): 9781789545708

Typeset by Adrian McLaughlin

Printed and bound in Great Britain by
CPI Group (UK) Ltd, Croydon CR0 4YY

Head of Zeus Ltd
5–8 Hardwick Street
London EC1R 4RG
WWW.HEADOFZEUS.COM

At the
Jerusalem

Introduction

In his poem 'The Old Fools', Philip Larkin imagines old age:

> Perhaps being old is having lighted rooms
> Inside your head, and people in them, acting.
> People you know, yet can't quite name, each looms
> Like a deep loss restored…

Paul Bailey's novel *At the Jerusalem* is both a portrait of the dissolving mind of an old woman and a display of pure style. The novel is mainly dialogue, with a cacophony of voices in a home for elderly ladies. Each has her own personal ailment; each is amused or annoyed by different things; each is ready to interject, demand attention, make jokes, slobber at meals, drool while pretending to listen, offer insults, fall asleep, become noisy in the night, have bad dreams, entertain old memories, take out false teeth.

Among the voices comes the sound of what is not being said, what appears as memory, or as a remark that might be made but is being withheld. In general, this sound belongs to Mrs Faith Gadny, the most recent arrival at the Jerusalem.

Mrs Gadny has, as Larkin puts it, a lighted room inside her head. While the others have become accustomed to the Jerusalem, she notices with all the intensity of a newcomer. And she experiences the memory of her husband and her daughter with more urgency than any of the voices that she hears around her. Her husband and daughter are like a deep loss restored.

The memory of her stepson Henry and his ghastly wife Thelma is made more present by their visit. Up until recently, Mrs Gadny has been living with them, but then they decided that it would be better for everyone if she were moved to a home. Also, Mrs Gadny imagines that her old friend Mrs Barber is still alive – she isn't – and she writes her forlorn letters.

The tone Paul Bailey wields with such skill and control in the novel is dry and brisk and distant, understated and filled with implication and irony. He writes sharp sentences and manages to make the reader not know quite what to feel. When Miss Trimmer, for example, one of the inmates, is performing her ablutions, she gets soap in her eye. There is much fuss. And, then, to end the scene and this section of the book, Bailey writes: 'After shaking some talcum powder into her knickers, Miss Trimmer dressed.' (p. 25)

The novel is a high-wire act, with not a sound or a piece of dialogue left unchiselled, not a false note. It moves from registering the most mundane activities – small arguments, communal meals, walks in the garden, talks with Matron –

with relish and impetus to entering into Mrs Gadny's mind with empathy and a kind of sympathy.

Mrs Gadny is easily bored and irritated. She really does want to be let alone, especially by Mrs Capes, who seeks to befriend her. The dead speak to her more and more. Scenes from the past come to torment her; she has bad dreams. She is becoming a difficult patient, neither too frail to be fully pitied nor sociable enough to enter into the general cheery spirit of the Jerusalem.

Bailey handles Mrs Gadny's losing her mind with subtlety; he integrates the ebb and flow of her consciousness with waves of good sense and ordinary appetites. It isn't that he normalizes her dementia; rather, he makes everyday speech and everyday patterns of activity in the novel so brittle and weird that Mrs Gadny's failing mind seems merely another aspect of the way things are.

The minimalism in the novel, so edged and barbed, has some of the same textures as scenes in *Waiting for Godot*, scenes in which lines of dialogue are repeated until they seem strangely resonant or oddly nonsensical, or in which banality holds sudden sway until the most ordinary remark or question can have a shivering aura. Bailey's use of short, clipped sentences and quickly moving dialogue with much repetition also takes its bearing from a tradition in English fiction that runs from Ronald Firbank through Ivy Compton-Burnett to Muriel Spark, fiction in which the reader is spared unnecessary detail, where the dialogue is sharply inconsequential until it suddenly becomes outlandishly comic or completely shocking. Nothing seems to be happening until a sentence or a line of dialogue swoops down on you, the gentle reader.

Since *At the Jerusalem* was published in 1967, the elderly residents would have been born in the Victorian age when many of them worked as servants. While a few inmates can be vulgar, others are prudish, not least Mrs Gadny herself. She thinks of her stepson and his wife involved in conjugal coupling with something less than equanimity: 'She suddenly imagined him on top of Thelma, misbehaving himself. How could *she*, scarcely more than a bean-pole, suffer all that weight?' (p. 111)

While many episodes in the book move between the funny and the sad, there are other scenes that are brilliantly and openly comic. Mrs Hibbs's ninetieth birthday is one such scene, the celebration not helped by the fact that Mrs Hibbs is herself more or less asleep and cannot be easily woken, even by 'a trickle of sherry' (p. 199). All around her there is good cheer, the sort that would make you want to weep.

Paul Bailey does nothing obvious to make us like Mrs Gadny or want her not to suffer. She shuts out the world of the Jerusalem, her universe is increasingly circumscribed, as she herself is less and less amenable to kindness and care. She is seldom funny and often irascible. She gives the nurses a bad time. Yet slowly, the more her mind dims, the more she emerges as fully present in the novel. Because she is not predictable, because her suffering is never exaggerated or sentimentalized, then she is a memorable protagonist, a character whose feelings and experience seem increasingly complex and demand close attention.

The structure of the novel helps us to see Mrs Gadny and her predicament clearly. It moves from her daily life at the Jerusalem back to her efforts to live with her stepson and his wife. Rather than offering high drama, Bailey dramatizes small moments of pure tedium, moments that exude minuscule forms of pain that slowly add up to an urgent need for Mrs Gadny's departure.

It is hard to think of another novel about an elderly character not in full possession of her wits that is written with the same amount of compassion and sensitivity. Bailey's genius in this book was to find a style supple enough to contain the tragedy befalling his heroine but also ambiguous enough to suggest a great deal about her mind and how it moves as it begins to fail her.

COLM TÓIBÍN, 2019

For my mother

Part One

Then there was a dazzle of green and white, white and green. Then the colours separated, became clear: the white was above, the green below. Tile, she saw, followed tile. Once she'd blinked, she realized that she stood in a corridor.

The nurse, who had walked some paces ahead of her, stopped and called: 'Mrs Gadny, you must come with me.'

Mrs Gadny moved towards the nurse, who smiled.

'Matron's waiting to welcome you.'

So they walked together along the corridor: the nurse looking at Mrs Gadny, Mrs Gadny staring ahead.

A window to Mrs Gadny's right gave her a view of the grounds at the back of the Home. She was surprised to see that there were graves. She walked to the window and looked out. Beyond the graves, women were seated on benches, enjoying the sun. One woman's skirt was drawn up above her knees, which shone in the strong light.

The nurse said gently: 'We won't stay cheerful – will we? – if we stare at the graveyard. Even though it's a pleasant sight on a fine day like this: the white stones and all the flowers. You come with me, Mrs Gadny. Matron's waiting to welcome you.'

But Mrs Gadny continued to stare. The sun shone on the graves, the women, the pair of knees. Like the tiled walls, they became confused before her. She had to blink to make certain that a gravestone wasn't grinning.

'The two of you will have a long talk. A nice chat, dear. Woman to woman.'

The nurse guided her forward.

'Smile. Let yourself smile. She's human, Matron. A widow like yourself. Her name's Mrs Ricks. You'll find her sympathetic, full of warmth.'

The nurse decided that a little humour would set Mrs Gadny's mind at rest. 'I'm Nurse Trembath,' she said, hoping her companion would smile. 'Some people find the name amusing. It isn't a common name, is it – Trembath? One of the ladies who used to be here hooted with laughter whenever she heard my name. She roared. It kept her happy.'

Mrs Gadny, the nurse noted, was not amused, as the expression went about Queen Victoria.

'And you'll be happy in no time. Oh, yes. I can see you don't believe me. Just wait. You'll settle. You'll grow accustomed.'

Nurse Trembath led her into another corridor.

'It's a big event – isn't it? – at your age. An upheaval. Almost as if you were starting a new life.'

She tightened her grip on Mrs Gadny's left hand.

'In a way, it *will* be a new life: the comfort, the care, the friends you'll have about you.'

They stopped at a dark-green door. Nurse Trembath said 'We're here' and knocked, listened, knocked again.

'Not a sound. She must be on her travels. I'll take you in, Mrs Gadny. You can sit and wait for her. Open, Sesame,' Nurse Trembath said.

She took Mrs Gadny into the Matron's office.

She sat and waited. A fly buzzed near her face. It landed on her nose. She didn't bother to brush it away. It pulled in its wings and rested. She closed her eyes.

'You have a fly on your nose.'

She heard a sharp voice. Turning in the chair, she saw a tall woman in a white dress. The tall woman leaned towards her; she brushed the fly away; she smiled as she said 'Good morning'.

Mrs Gadny attempted to rise.

'Remain in your seat. Good morning.'

'Good morning,' Mrs Gadny managed.

'And what a good morning it is. Wouldn't you agree?'

'Yes.'

'That sun out there. The birds.'

'Yes.'

The matron drew herself up; walked to her desk; sat behind it. 'Are you nervous? Do I frighten you?'

'No.'

'Am I an ogre?' She corrected herself. 'Ogress?'

'No.'

'You're wearing a very pretty hat.'

'Thank you.'

'It's most becoming.' The matron smiled, shut the smile off quickly. 'Shall we have tea? Would you like some tea?'

'Thank you.'

'Tea *would* be pleasant.' The matron picked up the telephone, spoke into it. 'Tea, please. For two.' She put down the receiver. 'Mrs Gadny.'

'Yes.'

'Tell me your Christian name. Or names.'

Mrs Gadny thought this strange. Henry must have filled in papers; he must have told this woman about her. She said, 'Faith Ethel.'

'Raise your voice.'

'Faith Ethel.'

'Faith Ethel. Yes.' She smiled, shut the smile off quickly. 'I have the facts about you here. I shan't need to ask you questions.'

The fly settled on Matron's bun.

'We can talk together. Over tea.'

Mrs Gadny watched the fly; saw there were grey streaks in Matron's hair.

'Smile.'

Mrs Gadny smiled. Matron smiled, shut off the smile quickly.

'How was your journey here?'

'All right. Thank you.'

'How did you travel? Train?'

'My stepson brought me. He drove me. He has a car.'

'So you arrived in style?'

'Yes. Yes.'

The fly set off again. Silence, apart from its buzzing. Matron sighed.

'You mustn't be sad. The Jerusalem's your home now.'

With green and white tiles, with graves.

'I understand your sadness. These last few hours must have been terrible for you. A terrible wrench.' Matron stopped. She spoke in a quieter voice: 'After so many years... I do realize. Believe me. Do believe me, Mrs Gadny. You'll be at ease. You'll settle. Adapt.'

The fly was on the window.

'Think of me as a friend.'

'Yes.'

'I am quite sincere. As a friend.' She was emphatic. 'I may be Matron but I'm also Mrs Ricks, another woman like yourself. If you find you have troubles, you must bring them to me. Without hesitation.' She smiled, shut the smile off quickly. 'Nothing's so dreadful it can't be talked about.'

'No.'

'Nothing. Remember.'

'Yes.'

'Your hands are clutching the chair. Look.'

'Oh? Yes.'

'Be comfortable. Sit back.'

'Yes.'

'I'm not commanding you.'

'No.'

Matron laughed, so Mrs Gadny smiled.

*

Tea was served from a trolley by a Nurse Perceval. There were biscuits and a cake.

'Take a plate, Mrs Gadny,' Matron said.

'I couldn't eat. I couldn't.'

'Couldn't?'

'I couldn't.'

'Not some cake?'

'No, thank you.'

'Have this wafer. It's thin.'

'I—'

'There you are.'

'Thank you.'

Nurse Perceval placed a cup of red tea on the desk in front of her.

Matron was a noisy drinker.

'Most people find our name curious.'

'Name?'

'The Jerusalem.'

'Oh?'

'You find it curious?'

'Yes. Very unusual.'

'New arrivals always ask me how it came about.'

'Do they?'

'How we acquired such an extraordinary title.' Matron smiled, shut the smile off quickly. 'All my ladies were intrigued by the story.'

They looked at each other.

'Would it interest you? The story?'

Mrs Gadny could not say 'No'.

'Yes.'

'Really? Truly?'

'Yes.' Matron still looked at her. 'Yes.'

'Did you notice the bust in the entrance hall?'

'I can't say I did.'

'It's in a prominent position. It's rather imposing.'

'I don't think I *did* notice.'

'Ah, well. It will strike your eye some time.'

In the future.

'It represents our founder, the bust. Lord Endon. He lived from 1857 to 1888. Not a long life and not a happy one.'

'Thirty-one years.'

'Very bright, Mrs Gadny. Very bright of you… However, to go on…'

Lord Endon, Matron told her, had a wretched childhood. Both his parents died before he was ten. He was a lord at nine and a half. An uncle then took charge of him: a man of loose morals who drank and gambled. By the time Lord Endon inherited his father's fortune, he himself was a drunkard. He had wasted his youth in low dens and such places. (Here Matron smiled.) At the age of twenty-eight His Lordship, on an impulse, went to the East. In 1885 he saw the Light. In Jerusalem. He returned to England to spread the Word. He lived among the London poor. He bought a property, a workhouse

7

at the time, and made it into a home for the elderly and dying. He called it the Jerusalem.

'Which is how we began.'

'What made him die?'

'A fever. He'd caught it on his journeys.'

'I see.'

Matron said there was more to tell, a good deal more, but it would keep, it would do for some other occasion. She told Mrs Gadny to drink her tea. She asked Nurse Perceval to fetch Mrs Capes.

'Mrs Capes is what you'd call a "character". She's energetic, has a lively mind. You'll take to her. She will amuse you, I can promise. Another wafer?'

'No. Thank you.'

'I shall ask her to guide you round the Home: show you all the nooks, all the crannies. And she can introduce you to the other residents, describe their little ways.'

Mrs Gadny shivered, despite the heat.

'Are you cold?'

'Oh no.'

'I was telling you about Mrs Capes.'

'Yes.'

'But you will see her.'

'My first name's Louise,' said Mrs Capes. '"Louise" is French.'

This was a new corridor. Brown tiles here.

'What shall I call *you*?'

'Faith.'

'Faith. When I was first here, Faith, I thought the place was all corridors. There seemed so many.'

'Oh?'

'One after another.'

At least they walked at a human pace. She'd been winded with the nurse.

'W.C.s.' Mrs Capes pointed at a door and smiled. 'Six of them.'

She opened the door. Six cubicles, painted brown on the outside; a basin; a towel-rack; black-and-white lino.

'Like any others. But we've more upstairs. Nicer ones. Brighter ones.'

Someone pulled a chain.

'Who's in there?'

'Me.'

And a little woman came out of the nearest cubicle. She wore an old scarlet dress, trimmed with lace, and a mangy tippet. She seemed like a hunchback, she was so bent over.

'This is Mrs Affery,' Mrs Capes said. 'Mrs Affery, Mrs Gadny.'

'How d'you do?' Mrs Affery smiled. She had no teeth. Her lips moistened as she spoke.

'How do you do?'

'Pleased to meet you. Nice to know you. Glad to see you.'

Mrs Gadny nodded, smiled.

The three women stood in the doorway, smiling. When the cistern gave its final hiss, Mrs Affery said:

'Goodbye.'

'Goodbye.'

No one moved. Mrs Gadny thought for a daft moment that Mrs Affery needed winding up.

Should she say 'Goodbye'?

But Mrs Capes did instead, in a very bright voice that set Mrs Affery into immediate motion. When she reached the corner, she turned and waved.

'She's a character.'

Mrs Gadny hadn't seen her wash her hands, and said so.

'She's forgetful. She leaves her teeth in the oddest places. Do you wish to visit before we move on?'

'No. Thank you.'

They walked to the end of the corridor.

'Mrs Affery has dreams.'

'Everyone has them.'

'Not like hers. Hers are terrible. The times she's woken screaming.'

They were in another corridor.

'You chose your day well. The weather couldn't be lovelier.'

'No.'

'The day I arrived, snow was on the ground and it was dark as dark. Thick of winter. I was so upset, too – coming here. I had everything against me. Look at me now, though – happy.' She laughed. 'I'm a cheerful soul.'

'Are you?'

'Why be gloomy? That's my motto. Isn't it yours?'

'Yes.'

'Why be gloomy? A question we should all ask ourselves.

Every morning when we rise; every night before sleeping. That's one of my beliefs.'

The next time she spoke, it was to indicate the lounge, which was empty. The ladies were all taking the sun, Mrs Capes explained.

'Most of us gather here of a night to watch TV. We follow our serials, we enjoy a play. It's a boon, isn't it, the TV?'

'Yes.'

'A boon. Poor Mrs Hibbs and poor Miss Burns, they never see it. We don't have a set in the ward and they're both confined to their beds. It *is* a shame.' She added, in a whisper: 'The life's out of them; they'd be better gone. The way they are, living's a burden for them. But that's only my view. And you can do without my views, can't you?' She took Mrs Gadny's right hand, patted it. 'Don't answer. It'll only be the truth.'

Mrs Capes laughed; Mrs Gadny smiled.

There was a green leather sofa and six green leather arm-chairs. There was a walnut table by the window. On the table was a bowl of daffodils. You could tell they were imitations because they hadn't been dusted.

'Shall we move on?'

'Yes. Thank you.'

'There's more to show you.'

Mrs Gadny made her hand slide free.

'Where we eat.'

They stood in a long hall.

'According to Matron, this is where *they* used to eat. By "they" I mean the paupers. What was it they ate? Gruel…'

She saw a trestle table, chairs on either side.

'And up there, up on that balcony—'

A balcony!

'—was where the workhouse master used to watch to see that they ate it. Their gruel.'

'DO NOT SPIT. MATRON.' was in a frame on the far wall.

'At Christmas we hang up streamers; we put up bunting. Ever so festive, it looks in here. And we have singsongs. A man comes in and builds a little stage and we each of us do a turn. I usually oblige with a song or two. By popular request.' Mrs Capes laughed. 'Matron plays the piano. She has a beautiful touch.'

'It sounds pleasant.'

'It is. A very happy occasion. As you'll see.'

'Yes.'

'This year perhaps *you* can sing for us—'

'Oh no.'

'Oh yes. Oh yes.'

'I can't sing. I've never been able to.'

Celia could.

'Never?'

'Never.'

'We don't expect Clara Butt. You don't have to be wonderful.'

Had she seen 'DO NOT SPIT. MATRON.'? She had. It was from when they'd had men in the Home, Mrs Capes told her. People had been too lazy to take it down.

The painted brick walls would have suited a prison more. And she could imagine rats appearing at night.

'We'll all be eating here at lunch-time. Eating our haddock.'

Mrs Capes had her hand again and was whispering:

'I must warn you now, Faith dear, in good time, that one or two of the ladies – ladies! – don't eat at all daintily. One or two of them slobber. So you keep your eyes screwed on your fish if that kind of thing upsets you. It upset me when I was new. I starved for days. And the noises they make!' Then she said 'Smile.'

Mrs Gadny smiled.

'I'll sit by you.'

'Thank you.'

'A pleasure. A person needs support at such a time. We'll be friends, that's a certainty.'

'Yes.'

'One more call.'

Mrs Capes gripped her hand and led her out.

They'd climbed stair after stair before Mrs Capes showed Mrs Gadny the nicer, brighter lavatories. Mrs Capes announced that they'd come to the end of the trail as they went into the ward.

'Those stairs,' said Mrs Gadny.

'Those stairs. As you say.'

The ward was as long as the hall. It was lighter, though. There were four big windows.

The stairs had worn her out. 'Let me catch my breath.'

Ten beds. Two of them occupied.

Mrs Capes said, 'There's the pair I told you of. Her asleep is Mrs Hibbs.'

Mrs Hibbs slept: her head dangling, mouth open. Mrs Capes said 'Good morning' to Miss Burns. Miss Burns sat upright, staring. She made no reply.

'Never seems to hear, never answers... This is a new lady: Mrs Gadny... Speak to the wall, you'd get more response.'

Lockers between the beds, like a hospital.

'Shall I tell you who goes where?'

'Yes. Please.'

'Well... This bed's Mrs Affery's – she's the one who came out of the closet.' Mrs Gadny nodded. 'Next to her's Miss Burns, who you see; in the middle there's Mrs Temple's; other side of her's Mrs Gross and the one in the corner's mine. This side of ward we have Mrs Hibbs, who's off in the Land of Nod this minute: she's opposite me. Old Mrs Crane's alongside her. There you'll find Mrs O'Blath. Irish, Mrs O'Blath. Laughs.' Mrs Capes seemed to disapprove. 'In the bed here it's Miss Trimmer.'

'And this is mine?'

'As ever was.' Mrs Capes laughed. 'One of my expressions.'

Mrs Gadny sat on her bed.

'I'd lie right down on it if I were you. See if it's to your liking.'

She lay down. A fly-paper hung from a white light-shade.

'Soft enough?'

'Yes.'

'You don't sound happy.'

'I *am* used to a hard bed. It *is* what I'm accustomed to.'

Since a child in the country. Her father held it that hard beds toughened you.

'I don't wish to complain—'

'We'll tell Matron. We'll go to her, you and me, and we'll state your requirements.'

'I don't wish to—'

'If it's for the best, it's what must be done.'

'As long as there's no—'

'None at all.'

'—trouble.'

'None at all.' Mrs Capes made her voice sound firm. 'That locker's for your bits and pieces, your worldly goods. If you have coats and dresses you want hanging up, there's a big wardrobe in that corner.' It was walnut, as was the table in the lounge. 'If you've brought your tiara, I'd advise you to hide it under the bed. You can keep it in the china.' She waited for Mrs Gadny's laugh. 'The thing with the flowers on it is a screen. You pull it round for emergencies. Like if you have to use what I just mentioned.'

She sat on a pillow near Mrs Gadny's head. 'Mrs Temple's never off it. Half the night. And you'd think it was the Niagara Falls.' She laughed loudly, as if to compensate for the silence that had followed her previous joke. 'That's my vulgar streak showing itself. It comes out now and again. What's life without honest dirt?' As she asked the question she saw two suitcases on the other side of the bed. 'Shall I help you unpack?'

'No, thank you. I can do it later.'

'As you please… Do you have photos?'

'Yes.'

'Of yourself and family?'

'Yes.'

'I've photos too. We must have a photo session. Does that appeal?'

'Yes.'

Mrs Gadny closed her eyes.

'Louise,' Mrs Capes said.

'Louise.'

'Shall we go down now and speak to Matron? Then, afterwards, we can sit in the sun.'

Descending the stone stairs, Mrs Capes asked Mrs Gadny if she'd been 'treated to a history lesson'.

'She mentioned a lord.'

'I'm sure she did.'

She heard herself say, 'I didn't want to hear about him.'

'No one does,' said Mrs Capes.

Miss Trimmer said, 'Look at the fools. Listen to them.'

The fools were applauding a blonde singer.

'If they'd clap for her they'd clap for me. Or anyone.'

Mrs Gadny was pressed between Mrs Capes and Mrs Affery on the sofa.

'The stars aren't what they were,' said Mrs Capes. 'Not at all, they're not.'

Mrs Crane mentioned Dan Leno.

'Ah!'

'I saw his Widow Twankey. He did a dance in clogs.'

The blonde singer blew kisses.

'Or Little Tich,' Mrs Crane continued. 'He springs to mind.'

'Little Tich. Yes!'

Mrs Capes had once seen Nellie Wallace. Mrs Crane sang a line or two of 'By the old blasted oak'.

'She was vulgar, yes, but funny.'

'Laugh!'

Mrs Temple had loved Harry Champion. And, she added, George Robey.

Mrs Gross said 'Gertie Ghana'.

'And her!'

As the blonde singer prepared herself for further song, Mrs Gross said 'Kate Carney'. She laughed as Miss Trimmer sang the phrase 'Three pots a shilling'. Mrs Affery snored.

'There's the whale again. There she blows!'

Mrs Temple looked pleased as everyone laughed.

Mrs Capes asked Mrs Gadny if she was comfy.

'Yes. Very. Thank you.'

'Settle yourself. You seem on edge.'

'Do I?'

Nurse Perceval opened the door and told them it was cocoa time.

At dawn she decided to write a letter.

My dear Mrs Barber. It is a long time since I wrote I know but much has been happening to me so that I havent had the time to sit down and put pen to paper, it must be a year since we last heard from each other, I hope you are well. How is your home. Cornwall must be beautiful now if the weather here is anything to go by, I am still in one piece (T.G.) but for how much longer I cant say.

The birds were deafening.

One thing I do like is to write a letter as well you know, it gives me pleasure, all my life Ive enjoyed sending letters and getting them back, but not this past year.

She calmed herself.

The trouble started last july, my Celia took to her bed, the doctor called and looked at her and said she was a puzzle, he said she would have to go to a hospital as it was a complete mystery to him what was the matter with her.

Miss Burns was staring.

So she went and we soon found out it was a disease of the blood, I wont put the word down as I cant spell it but it begins with a L.

She prided herself on being able to spell most words.

She got so white my Celia she would have been taken for a ghost, she who had always been healthy, always running about, always active, even from a girl. The flesh went from her, in the end she was like a stalk, she died in january and I cant deny it was a release. Her funeral was quiet, she had few friends.

That would upset Mrs Barber.

What happens happens I suppose, with Celia gone there was only a pension to support me, I didnt expect any help from my stepson (Henry you remember he was by Toms first) but he came to see me and asked me if I would like to stay with him and his wife, so I went, I was a fool to go, they found me moody, hard to please and Thelma (Henrys wife) said I upset the children. What they have done is this, they have found me a place in a home, it is called the jerusalem home, it used to be a workhouse as one glance would show. It is for old ladies though they did once have men as well.

She made a space and wrote:

I have been disposed of. It is morning as I write, I have spent my first night here and I cant say I have slept, I am in a ward with 9 others and some of them are a sorry sight, I shall try to keep them out of my mind. There is a matron here and nurses, the matron is one of those women who smile, I have never trusted women who smile, that is my nature.

She would have to end. The tall one, Miss Trimmer, was awake.

> I will write again Mrs Barber in due course, I rely on you to answer me to tell me about your kind family who look after you and the sea and the beach and the wonderful views, you write a good letter, a few words from you will take me away from here in the spirit, I remain Your Good Friend,
>
> F. E. GADNY (MRS)

She would write the envelope later and she'd ask a nurse to post it.

'Dear, dear, Faith. Whatever's up?'

Mrs Capes found her weeping.

'I was looking for you. I've searched high and low.'

She was curled up like a baby on the bed.

'I thought we could have tea together. We can take it outside in the sun. There's tables.'

Mrs Gadny looked at Mrs Capes.

'The doctor.'

'The doctor? Doctor Gettrup?'

'The lady doctor.'

'That's Doctor Gettrup. What's she done?'

'I said I didn't want her to see me. I told her I'm used to a man doctor, that's what I'm accustomed to. I told Matron if she wanted to know my state of health to fetch Doctor Bicknall, 22 Painter Street – I've been on his books for fifteen years. She wouldn't listen. She told me to do what the lady doctor said.'

Doctor Gettrup had told her to remove her clothes.

'In that room. With the smell of disinfectant.'

She'd asked the doctor and the nurse – it was the one called Barrow – to look away.

The nurse pulled down the window-blind.

Eventually, she was naked.

'I was naked, Mrs Capes.'

'Louise, dear.'

'Louise.'

Her breasts, which had never been large enough, drooped. Her belly stuck out. The tops of her legs were dark with veins.

'She kept touching me. As if I was a thing. I was naked. With that woman staring.'

'Wipe your eyes. It's over. Let's take tea.'

She'd covered a certain place with both hands.

'Tea's the remedy for everything. Come on, Faith dear, come with me.'

'Yes. Yes, I will. What a fool I am, snivelling. I feel ashamed.'

'A cry does you good. That's one of my beliefs. A nice cry does you good.'

Matron advised the nurses to humour her.

'I must confess I was amused when she objected to a woman

seeing her naked. "I'm used to a man," she said.' She blushed at her impersonation but the nurses laughed.

'Doctor was tickled, too,' Nurse Barrow said.

'I can trust you all to be attentive to her, can't I?'

'Yes, Matron.'

'She thinks she's come to an institution. It's only natural that she should. I think it might be some little time before she's made the necessary adjustment. Until then, velvet paws.'

The nurses smiled.

'Mrs Capes has taken to her. She says she'll make her happy if it's the last thing she does.'

When she awoke from her doze in the sun, she had a headache and a sick taste in her mouth.

Mrs Capes was on the bench beside her, eyes closed. She had drawn up her skirt: hers were the shining knees.

Mrs Gadny would describe her to Mrs Barber, she would find words. There were the dinners, the tiles, the graves to write about. And the doctor with the peculiar name. She would spare Mrs Barber no detail of her humiliation.

News from Mrs Barber would bring some comfort.

Miss Trimmer and Mrs Gross always washed at six o'clock.

Mrs Gross dabbed herself lightly with a flannel. Water disagreed with her skin.

Miss Trimmer was very thorough. As well as baths, she stripped down to her knickers whenever she washed, cold weather or hot. She soaped an armpit as she said:

'Spare us another night like that.'

Mrs Gross, who was nothing like her name, but very thin and tiny, knew what her friend expected her to ask.

'Like what?'

'You didn't hear her?'

'Hear? Hear who?' 'Hear who?' sounded funny and Mrs Gross was about to laugh at the expression when Miss Trimmer said:

'Her. Mrs Gadny. All the bloody night, bloody crying. Sniff, sniff.'

She washed the soap away and sniffed under her left arm.

'I didn't hear her. I slept heavy.'

'Sniffing away. It played on my nerves, Nell, like a tap dripping. I couldn't settle, hard as I tried.'

'Poor creature.'

'Poor creature, my arse-hole. One kind of woman I can't bear, it's her kind.'

'She's unhappy, Edie.'

'We're all unhappy, Nell. The whole bleeding world's unhappy.'

'Edie—'

'I'm serious, whether you think I am or not. I mean what I said.' She set to work on her breasts: hoisted them higher, placed her left arm under them to maintain the position, sponged them with her right hand. 'Is she so special? Why should she be happy? Why her? And as she isn't, why doesn't she show some self-respect?'

The breasts fell back into place. She dried them carefully.

'You can be very harsh, Edie.'

'I know I can.'

'I'm sure, given time, she'll find herself at ease.'

'Are you? Will she?'

'Yes, Edie.' Mrs Gross smiled at her friend. 'You always think the worst.'

'Wisest policy, Nell. Much the wisest.'

'For you, it may be—'

'I'm talking for me. I can only talk for me.'

'Now you're being cantankerous, Edith.' She called her 'Edith' when she needed reprimanding. 'You're being an old cuss. Crack your face, Misery-guts. You talk about her, look at *you*.'

'Well,' said Miss Trimmer. 'Well.'

They continued their morning wash, in the upstairs washroom where the nicer, brighter lavatories were.

Mrs Gross finished her dabbing. Her body coped with, Miss Trimmer applied soap to her face. Soon she shrieked:

'Oh, bloody curses, I've blinded myself. Soap's in my eyes, Nell. Bring me my towel.'

'Yes.'

'Quick. Quickly.'

It took her a moment to find it. Miss Trimmer had thrown it on the scales.

'I said quickly. My eyes are burning. Don't be all day, Nell. Where've you gone for it, you moo – Land's End?'

'I'm coming, Edie. Be patient.'

'Patient, she says. Here I am, blinded—'

'You're not blinded and don't be so wicked. It's only soap.'

'It hurts.'

'Come on, push your head back. Put the towel to your eyes.'

Miss Trimmer could see again. 'The relief! Oh!'

For all her talk, Miss Trimmer was easily put out by things. Mrs Gross had to laugh.

'There's something in that soap, some chemical. My eyes feel as if they've had a poker stuck in them.'

'All soap hurts when you get it in your eyes.'

'Not like that did. It's cheap carbolic muck. I shall make a point of telling Matron.'

After shaking some talcum powder into her knickers, Miss Trimmer dressed.

'You can't manage beef without teeth, Maggy,' said Mrs Crane.

'What?'

'You need teeth to eat this meat. Something to chew with.'

'I've lost them. I've reported them missing.'

'You *are* careless.'

'I can't hear you. Your mouth's full of food.'

Mrs Temple asked Queenie Crane to pass the horseradish sauce.

'I'm sorry, Alice. I beg your pardon.'

Miss Trimmer wondered whether the cow had been drawing her pension at the time of her death. Or was it a bull?

Anyway, she reminded everyone present (and she looked at Nurse Barrow and Nurse Perceval as she spoke) that animals were being given chemicals. What they were all eating, or trying to, was not natural meat. She remembered what beef used to be like. So did Mrs Crane and Mrs Temple. Mrs Crane looked fierce when she said it was against God's will.

Mrs Gadny saw Mrs O'Blath laughing. Then everyone turned to look because she was shaking. Her chins, her breasts, her arms that had turned purple from the sun.

'She's started.'

Mrs Crane asked 'Why you laughing?'

'What's funny, Peggy?' Mrs Temple calculated that Mrs O'Blath had not laughed really loudly for three days.

'Peg, Peg—'

'You'll burst.' Mrs Crane was still fierce.

Tears came out of Mrs O'Blath's eyes.

'What's funny, Peggy?'

She pointed at Maggy Affery, from whose mouth a piece of gristle dangled.

'Look. Look.'

The gristle moved farther into the mouth, stopped.

'Her face. Look.'

The gristle disappeared. Mrs Affery's cheeks were working wildly.

'She's lost her teeth again,' Mrs Crane explained.

Mrs O'Blath's laugh soared higher.

'But she only found them yesterday.'

'The train robbers took them.'

Mrs Crane said: 'They're laughing at you, Maggy.'

'Eh?'

'They're laughing at you.'

'Oh? Are they? Not to worry.'

'Chop it up small. The meat.'

'Not a baby. I can eat all right.'

'I'd chop it up—'

'—if you were me.'

Mrs O'Blath's laugh descended the scale a fraction. 'I can't stop myself. I need some water, otherwise I'll choke.' She sipped at her glass of water. She patted her bosom. She returned to her meal.

The creature in the tippet had upset Mrs Gadny. She stared at her own two pieces of beef, her four greasy baked potatoes and her small mound of boiled cabbage.

'She makes me laugh so,' Mrs O'Blath was telling her. 'Maggy does make me laugh so.'

Mrs Gadny looked at Mrs Affery. Perhaps, if she willed it, she might laugh.

'Eat, Faith. Don't look at her.'

It wasn't a funny spectacle.

'Don't look,' said Mrs Capes.

'No.'

There was the food to deal with. Mrs Crane and Miss Trimmer had already dealt with theirs. Nurse Barrow collected their plates.

'It was delicious, Nurse Barrow,' Miss Trimmer said. 'Such a tender joint. Might I inquire what we're having to follow?'

'Semolina.'

'Do you hear that, girls? We're to have semolina.'

She had not yet slept in her bed although a hard mattress had been supplied. The sheets smelled of bleach. A rash appeared under her left rib: she spent her third night in the Jerusalem scratching.

Mrs Affery had woken the other ladies at three o'clock with her screaming.

'Louise. Louise. Louise. How many more times, Faith? You must call me Louise. If you want my friendship. Do you want it?'

'Yes, Louise.'

'Be honest with me. If you think I'm a nuisance, a wicked old chatterer, anything else – tell me. I promise not to take umbrage.'

'I *am* honest, Louise. I want your friendship.' She smiled wanly. 'Yes, I do.'

'And I want yours.'

Mrs Gadny had dozed. She had not slept during the night. Soon after dawn she'd placed herself in the lavatory, where it was cool and peaceful. Celia's face had come to her.

They sat together in the shade, near the grave of a Samuel Wormbey.

'Five days, Faith,' Mrs Capes reminded her.

'Five, yes.'

'Soon be fifty, then a hundred.'

This was the hottest June day for years. The sun was far too strong for bathing in. Mrs Capes's knees were covered.

Mrs Capes narrowed her eyes and asked: 'What do you think of them?'

'Who?'

'"Who?" she asks! The ladies. Ladies! Have you formed an opinion?'

'Not exactly.'

'Not exactly! I wager you have. I bet you could say some fine things already.'

'Oh no.'

A bird landed on Samuel Wormbey's grave.

'That bird. What is it?'

'A thrush.'

'Look at him. See how he's got that worm. Pouncing and pecking away.'

'They have a lovely song, thrushes.'

'All birds sound the same to me.'

'Their song's lovely.'

Mrs Capes's stomach made a noise.

'Did you hear? My stomach rumbled.'

'No.'

One didn't mention body noises.

'Pardon. That was it again. I don't wonder it's making noises – after that meal.' Boiled bacon, pease pudding, spring greens. Mrs Capes belched. 'Pardon.'

'Granted.'

They smiled at each other. The bird flew away. 'Something I noticed, Louise, the day I came: I meant to ask you about it. Or Matron.'

'Ask me.'

'I *did* notice, when I was in the toilet—'

'When you were on the toilet – yes?'

'While I was in the toilet, I noticed there was no lock on the door. I had to keep it shut with my foot. None of the doors have locks, have they?'

'No. For a good reason, Faith.'

Mrs Gadny waited for the good reason but Mrs Capes stayed silent.

Was Mrs Gadny in suspense? Mrs Capes was sure she was, so she said: 'There's a story attached, actually.' She paused.

'What story?' Mrs Gadny asked.

'I won't tell you.' Then: 'I won't tell you because it's not what you'd call cheerful.'

'Tell me the reason.'

'I couldn't—'

'Please.' She was almost excited.

'I warn you, dear.'

'Tell me. Tell.'

'Yes, dear. All right.'

Mrs Capes waited until Mrs Gadny's fingers had stopped drumming on the arm of the bench. She wanted complete attention. She began: 'There was a woman here once, she was called Belle Waters. She was a big person, blowzy, she'd been a barmaid, had the look about her. She stayed beautiful for a long while: you could see how she must have been. And she always cared for her appearance, took great pains. Especially her bosom: her old tits got dusted every day.'

What a picture.

'Then – it was sudden – she let herself go. The nurses had to wash her, she grew so dirty. All the spirit left her. She sat about and stared. Similar to Miss Burns, but worse because she looked as though she still had some life in her. She got so, they had to feed her; it was such an effort for her to eat. You may wonder, Faith, what this has to do with your question.'

'I do wonder rather.'

'Here's the answer. Belle Waters hanged herself on a lavatory chain. Yes, she did. Of all the places to end it!'

It was an effort, but she laughed.

'I haven't made out to this day how she found the energy.'

'Hanged?'

'Nurse Trembath discovered her. She took it well, never showed what a shock it must have given her. What a week that was. We had our names in the papers. There was a snap of me in one of them wearing my black costume at her funeral. Over it they'd put "HER OLD FRIEND MOURNS".' She underlined the words in the air. 'I've the cutting with my photos. You'll see it. It's a nice likeness even though the day it was taken it was very cloudy and the man had trouble with the light.'

Hanged.

*

She pulled up her knees under the sheets and placed her writing-pad on them.

My dear Mrs Barber. It is me again writing to you, I can just imagine what you will say when this letter arrives on your mat, it is her again, that is what you will say.

Are you well. I began to wonder today as I have not received your reply, I hope you are in the best of health, you cant be wanting for fresh air. But I so hope you are not ill and my writing to you a burden.

I have now been here 5 days and nights, I have settled as much as I ever shall, the people here are not of my kind, I mean nothing spiteful by that, it is the truth. There is one woman a Mrs Capes (C or K I dont know) who has been friendly but I think she is ruled by pity and that makes me wary of her. I may be wrong, I shall be glad to be for once, but I do not think she is genuine, not like you Mrs Barber or like my Tom or Celia. The way they have all been at me you would have taken me for a freak, they kept telling me to smile, every other word was smile, if I had smiled as often as they wanted me to I would have ended up as a Cheshire Cat. Yes as bad as that. I realise I have made a rime Mrs Barber but I am writing early so I can send this by the 1st post, please excuse mistakes.

I will write a full and proper letter when I have heard from you, I am dying to hear from you, my regards to your family my dear. Ever yours,

F. E. GADNY (MRS)

She addressed the envelope, sealed it.

She had not mentioned the dinners, the graves, the tiles, the doctor with the peculiar name, the humiliation.

They would keep.

Thelma had settled for the blue – it was right for the weather and suitable for the occasion. It would be catching with her new red hair.

She stared at her husband. Away from their home, Henry was always a stranger to her. He seemed happy, actually happy, reading the stones on graves.

'"Eliza, daughter of Mary and Joshua Phipson, both of this parish" – it says, Thelma – "in her twelfth year. May the tenth, 1867."'

She enjoyed the sun but not the heat.

'They said it would be hot today. I never thought as hot as this. I'm starting to perspire.'

She'd almost said 'sweat'.

'"Samuel Wormbey, aged ninety-five and seven weeks. Rest in Peace." He must have been a midget, a dwarf, by the size of his grave.'

'Today of all days it has to be this hot. Next week, when we're at the seaside, I can see it pouring. As it did last time.'

'"Rose Barley, in childbirth."'

'We'll be sitting there, in that front room, looking out at the rain.'

'No, we won't. Listen to this one. "Martha Rendell, Content to Rest in the Lord, Christmas Day, 1890."'

'Must you read out those things? They give me the willies.'

'Why should they do that?'

'They do. They're gloomy.'

'Silly girl, Thelma. We all come to it.'

'I don't wish to be reminded, thank you all the same. In this heat, to read those things!'

'What's the heat to do with it?'

She knew what it had to do with it but couldn't say. And Henry was smiling in an annoying manner. His mouth had twisted on one side.

'They don't even have nice verses.'

'This place was for the poor. Verses were expensive.'

Now he was correcting her.

He told her how fortunate Miss (or Mrs) Barley, Mr Wormbey and the others buried behind the Jerusalem were: a century earlier (less) they'd have been dumped into a communal grave. A hole, Henry said, and they were tipped from carts. He mentioned the smell and Thelma shivered. He was elated: he talked of fevers, plagues; ailments – like colds and toothache – which ended lives. At home he'd stay quiet for hours: you had to scream sometimes to get him to speak to you, to answer the simplest question.

'Look at that woman staring,' Thelma said.

A tall woman seated on a bench with a little woman had fixed her eyes on Thelma.

'She's curious,' Henry answered.

'Let's move away.'

They walked in the direction of the Home.

'Perhaps she's refused to see us, Henry.' Thelma was hopeful.

'She wouldn't do that.'

They were out of the graveyard now.

Mrs Gadny stood in the doorway, blinking.

Henry waved to her. 'Hullo,' he called.

When they were near her, Thelma said, 'Hullo, dear.'

Thelma had red hair.

'Hullo.'

She must have dyed it in celebration.

'Keeping well?' Henry asked.

'Yes.'

Thelma told her she looked well.

'Do I?'

'Oh, yes. Are they feeding you?'

'They are.'

'Plenty of fresh meat and vegetables?'

'Yes.'

'That's good.'

They were silent. Thelma blushed when Henry adjusted his trousers at the crotch. 'Shall we all sit down?' she asked loudly.

'Yes.'

'Where shall we sit ourselves, dear?'

'On a bench.'

'Any particular one? Do you have a special?'

'No.'

'I'm sure you will have in time.'

They sat on either side of her.

'This weather, it could be tropical. The car coming was like an oven. An oven, wasn't it, Henry?'

'Very hot.'

'I forced him to buy me this dress. Does it have your approval, dear?'

She said how pretty it was. An electric blue.

'Have you made any friends?'

'I speak to one or two of the ladies.'

'I suppose it *is* early yet.'

'Yes, it is.'

'Oh, aren't I forgetful? Here I am, dear, sitting with your present in my hands. These are for you. Assorted chocolates. I hope they haven't melted. Take them, dear. Eat them under the sheets tonight.' Thelma nudged her, laughed.

Assorted chocolates.

'When I was having Edna in the Samaritan I must have eaten hundreds of chocolates under the sheets at night. I didn't want the other patients to see how greedy I was.'

Mrs Gadny said 'Thank you'. She had to look ahead: Thelma smelled of some cheap perfume and Henry of sweat.

'I have a message to give you. From Edna and young Michael. They asked me especially to pass on their love.'

'That was thoughtful of them.'

'They *will* be excited this week, Michael and Edna, with their holiday coming up.'

'They will be.'

'I shall have a job keeping them under control.'

Henry removed his tie.

'Who's that woman staring?'

'Her name's Miss Trimmer.'

'Is she pleasant?'

'She has a sharp tongue. People say.'

'She looks as though she has. Is there something wrong with me? Am I showing something I shouldn't? Whatever it is, she makes me uncomfortable. Do you see her, Henry? If I hate anything, it's people staring at me. If she keeps on, I shall have words with her, I really shall. Perhaps she thinks I'm a leper.'

Henry saw Thelma covered in sores, shaking a bell. He smiled.

'There! She's stopped at last. We walked among the graves, dear, and her eye was on us then.'

Henry heard his stepmother's breathing: it made him conscious that his wife had stopped talking.

'Have you been able to sleep?'

'On and off.'

'You get your hot bath every day?'

'I do.'

Yes, I am clean.

Thelma crossed her legs, looked at Mrs Gadny, said: 'Those quarrels we had, dear, I hope you've begun to forget them. Our differences of opinion. History now, I hope.'

Henry closed his eyes.

'When you think, which I *have* been doing this past week,

37

you realize it *was* too much to expect that we should live happily together: not a sensible arrangement at all. I admit to you, dear, that I'm not an easy person to live with and Henry will bear me out, won't you?'

She did not expect an answer. She laughed, continued: 'To be serious for a moment or two – were we ever close, dear? We never were, were we? You and Celia, bless her, you both led such a simple, quiet life: it was a miracle wasn't it? – if we all met more than once in a year. We did hope, when you first came to us, that everything would be for the best – as well you know – but Fate thought otherwise, didn't she? I can't express myself, that's a gift I don't possess, but I think you may have gathered from what I've been saying that Henry and me – and I – we neither of us feel any ill will. Quite the reverse, to tell the truth. We really are very sorry, more than my words could ever convey.'

She waited for Mrs Gadny to speak.

No sound.

'And at your age, to have to cope with children – one barely grown. To have to listen to their chatter, keep patience with their ways – it isn't sensible.'

Thelma's voice cut your head to pieces. Let Henry speak – 'Hasn't Henry anything to say?'

'The heat's exhausted him.' Thelma laughed.

'I do feel dozy,' Henry said, his eyes still closed.

Mrs Gadny stood naked, her white belly stuck out. A doctor's cold hands touched her.

She spoke slowly. 'Whatever you say, Thelma, I've been disposed of.' An image came. 'Like trash, waste.'

'Now, dear, those words—'

'You aired your conscience. You can't escape the real truth. Can you? Can you?'

'Calm yourself. You are about to be hysterical.'

But she said in a quiet, steady voice:

'Trash, Thelma. Waste.'

Thelma could only say 'Now, now'.

Mrs Gadny knew she would cry. Her lower lip quivered. Henry and Thelma would imagine themselves the cause of her tears. Her own naked body had vanished: here was Celia now, crisp white sheet up to her chin, eyes the grey centres of black circles.

A fit of temper would blot the picture out. She turned her hands into fists and banged on the box in her lap.

'Have your bloody chocolates, Thelma. Have the bloody things.' She did not give them back. 'Is the inspection over? I can still stand, I still walk, I've eaten, I've slept, I've had bloody baths—'

She heard Celia cough.

'I don't want to speak to you.'

The cough came again. She wept whenever she heard it.

'I see.'

Sense was demanded. Henry, eyes open, asked her: 'Why do you cry?'

The noise grew uglier. He looked at her quickly and saw that her mouth was open, the throat visible. He concentrated on his dust-covered shoes.

'You were unhappy with us; you couldn't be unhappier

39

here. Think of those scenes every day, you and Thelma wearing each other down; think of those. Mop up your tears.'

Gasps of breath took over from the moaning. Henry could chalk up a victory. 'Come on,' he said.

Thelma suggested she try a chocolate.

Mrs Gadny opened the box. She put a chocolate in her mouth. It had a coffee flavour.

Henry told her she'd laugh at herself in time.

'Yes.'

She dabbed at her eyes and blew her nose.

'Use my compact,' Thelma said.

Thelma opened her handbag. She passed Mrs Gadny her compact. Mrs Gadny powdered her face.

'We can stay an hour, dear.'

Thelma shut her bag. They sat in silence.

Mrs Capes stood in front of them.

'It's tea-time, Faith dear.'

'Thank you.'

Mrs Capes waited for introductions.

'I'm Mrs Gadny's stepson. Henry Gadny. This lady is my wife Thelma.'

'My name is Capes. Mrs Louise Capes. How do you do?'

'How do you do?'

'How do you do?'

Mrs Capes wondered if they were staying for tea.

'Yes,' Henry said. 'Yes. We are,' Thelma added.

'Cook's made scones.'

*

'Move in a little, will you please, Mrs Capes?'

'How am I now?'

'Hold your tea cup. It looks more natural.'

Henry was posing them for a photograph. Thelma, Mrs Capes and Mrs Gadny sat in the dining-hall by a corner window. Tea things were on a card table.

Thelma told Mrs Capes: 'He took beauties at the seaside our last holiday. One of young Michael by his sandcastle and the funniest one of Edna with a lifebuoy round her middle at the end of the pier. He got her expression, he really did.'

Henry asked if they were ready.

'Are we?' Thelma and Mrs Capes were. 'Smile, dear... Please, dear, smile.'

'Come on, Faith. Be a sport.'

Thelma and Mrs Capes shared a look. Mrs Gadny smiled.

'Hold it.'

He took the photograph. 'Perfect.'

Miss Trimmer, who was having tea at the trestle table with the other woman, called to Henry, 'What about a picture of us, Mister? We're the lovely ones.'

Mrs Gross said 'Edie!'

'We'd win any contest. Especially our Maggy here.'

'Get in a group then.'

'D'you mean it?'

'She was only—' Mrs Gross started to say.

'Come on, girls, gather round.' Miss Trimmer clapped her

hands three times. 'The man's going to take our photo. You, Nell, and Queenie and Alice. Come along. Peggy. You sit by me, Maggy.'

Mrs Affery sat with Miss Trimmer at the table's head. To Mrs Affery's left, Mrs Temple and Mrs Crane; to Miss Trimmer's right, Mrs Gross and Mrs O'Blath.

'We're all together, Mister.'

'Smile.'

Smile.

Everyone smiled for him, except the lady with the fur, 'Would the lady with the fur smile, please?'

'Smile, Maggy,' Miss Trimmer said.

Maggy showed her gums. Mrs O'Blath couldn't contain herself.

'She's away.'

Mrs O'Blath said, 'Look at her. Look.'

Mrs Crane had her fierce face on. 'Stop it, Peggy. He only wants a smile.' Wouldn't her laughing mean a blur on the photograph?

Miss Trimmer told Mrs O'Blath that her tonsils could be seen.

Mrs Affery said to let her laugh.

'Are we all ready?' Henry asked.

'Ready.'

'We're ready.'

He took the photograph. 'There!'

Miss Trimmer wanted to know if he had got them all in.

'Yes.'

'You'll send us copies?'

'I will.'

'We'll pay you.'

'No, you won't. It's my pleasure.'

'Pleasure! What's he after?' Some of the women giggled. 'Well, thank you, Mister. We won't keep you any longer.' She had noticed Thelma, glaring. She gave her a sweet smile.

Henry returned to the card table. Thelma said, 'She was the woman who stared at me so rudely. She has a nerve.'

'I think it will be a good photo. If it turns out well, I might send it to a newspaper. Newspapers print unusual snaps.'

Mrs Capes poured Thelma the last cup in the pot and handed her the remaining scone.

'You have been very nice company, Mrs Capes.'

'And so have you. Both of you.'

Henry thanked her for saying so. He hoped they would all meet again.

'I'm sure we will.'

'You're very fortunate, dear, having Mrs Capes for a friend.'

'Yes.'

'Fortunate!' Mrs Capes protested. 'Are you fortunate, Faith?'

'Yes.'

'Shall we go, Henry?'

The afternoon had taken a pleasant course.

'We'd best be on our way.'

The children, Thelma said. They were seldom parted from their mother. Young Michael was inclined to bouts of crying. His had been a difficult birth.

'Faith and me, Faith and I rather, will see you off. We'll wave you goodbye from the steps. Won't we, dear?'

'Yes.'

Nurse Barrow was at the door of the dining-hall. Thelma nodded in a gracious manner as she passed.

Miss Trimmer said goodbye to Henry.

'Goodbye.'

Miss Trimmer told Mrs Affery to blow him a kiss. So Mrs Affery did, and everyone laughed.

'She's set her sights on you, young man.'

'Goodbye, Maggy.'

'Goodbye, Handsome.'

Thelma pulled at his sleeve. Miss Trimmer said, 'Goodbye, Lady.'

'Henry, come on.'

'Goodbye to you all.'

Voices followed them along the corridor:

'Goodbye.'

'Ta ta.'

'Go along, Henry.'

'Goodbye, Handsome.'

And laughter.

They passed Lord Endon and went out on to the steps.

The car moved slowly away. Mrs Capes returned Thelma's wave.

'Beautiful junket, Mrs Hibbs. Open now.'

Nurse Trembath opened Mrs Hibbs's mouth and gave her a spoonful of junket.

'Isn't it tasty? Miss Burns loved hers. Thoroughly enjoyed it.'

Miss Burns stared ahead.

The sky had gone a fantastic shade of purple. Wisps of white cloud floated across it.

Mrs Capes led Mrs Gadny into the ward.

'Find your photos, Faith dear. This minute.'

'Photos?'

'Yes. We can have the session we promised ourselves. Your son taking our picture reminded me.'

'Stepson.'

'Stepson, then.'

'Are you sure you want to see them?'

'Am I sure? You know the answer without my saying. I've kept mine in a book, have you yours?'

'No. I meant to once, but never did.'

'We'll sit on your bed – shall we? – and make an evening of it.'

It was decided.

Mrs Capes went to the foot of Mrs Hibbs's bed. 'Good evening, Nurse.'

'Good evening, Mrs Capes.'

'Enjoying your meal, Winnie?' Winnie Hibbs had a spoon in her mouth. 'I'll say she is,' Nurse Trembath said.

Mrs Gadny dragged a suitcase from under the bed. It contained her choicest underwear, Tom's Bible, some lavender in a cotton bag, a maid's cap and a pile of photographs.

She removed the photographs, closed the case, pushed it back. She placed the photographs on the bedspread. She wondered how she would get up again.

She rose somehow. Palms flat on the floor, behind high in the air, legs straightened. She thought the blood would rush out of her ears.

Her knees were dirty: two black rings. She shook the dust from her skirt.

Mrs Capes's book was dusty too. 'It hasn't seen daylight since I don't know how long. Like the best china, it only comes out on special occasions.' She brought the book level with her chin and blew the dust off.

They watched the cloud form, disintegrate.

'Beautiful junket.'

'Shall we do mine first?'

'Oh, it's beautiful.'

'Yes.'

'We could look at yours if you'd prefer.'

'Yours first would be best.'

'Whereabouts shall we park our fans?' Mrs Capes supplied her laugh. 'Me being vulgar again. The end of the bed – that'd be comfiest.'

Once they were seated, and Mrs Capes had spread herself and Mrs Gadny arranged her dress so that her veins weren't on view, the book was opened.

'LOUISE WATTS, HER BOOK.'

'Watts was my maiden name.'

'Yes.'

'Now… Where are we?… You can barely see these, Faith, they're so faded… Mother and Father. He seems all whiskers, doesn't he? Dundrearies, I believe they were called.'

'Yes. They were.'

'His name was Eph, short for Ephraim – I never heard anyone call him *that*. Mother was Martha. A lot of the family had Bible names. It was the custom those days.'

'Yes. It was.'

'Beautiful junket.'

'Where they found "Louise" from I don't know. I was thought something special when I was young on account of my name. Can you imagine?'

No. It would mean an effort.

'People I worked for in service, they all remarked on it. I must have been the only Louise in our part of Camberwell.'

Mrs Capes was thoughtful. 'Can you see my mother's face?'

'No.'

'Put the book nearer the light.'

She still couldn't see Mrs Capes's mother.

'The sky's a marvel.'

And it was. It was several shades of purple. The wisps of cloud might have been steps leading to heaven. The sun was a white ball in the top right-hand corner.

For a daft moment, she saw angels with trumpets. But the ward was silent, there were no hosannahs.

Mrs Capes had switched on the electric light.

'No angels.'

'What?'

'Nothing.'

Mrs Gadny looked at the book again.

'Can you make her out?'

'Not clearly.'

'Too faded. She was no beauty, she was the first to say so. She took snuff a good deal: she'd taken it for so long that when she was old all round her mouth was brown. Nigger colour.' Another joke, another laugh. 'What a character she was! She had hundreds of expressions.'

—Her book.

'Three more spoonfuls.'

'I'll turn the page, shall I?'

Yes, yes.

'These are me, these. God alone knows where they found the money for photos – we were a poor family, dear. Who wasn't poor then? Though I'll say this – we weren't as poor as some… I was an only, were you?'

'No.'

'Isn't it beautiful junket?'

'Her and her bloody junket… Aren't I wicked?'

Beautiful, beautiful junket.

'Where was I?'

'Only child.'

'Oh, yes. I say "only" but there *was* a brother born when I was two. He lived a month. This is him, naked on his blanket.'

Naked.

'Isn't it sad?'

'Yes.'

'Look at my long drawers in this one. And here I am paddling at Margate. Was it Margate or was it Morecambe? I can't recall. See my bucket, my spade?'

'Yes.'

'And my face, the smile on it. I was always smiling.'

'Were you?'

'The last little bit,' Nurse Trembath was heard to say.

'Oh, yes. Your son has a lovely smile, hasn't he?'

'Stepson.'

'Stepson. A lovely smile.'

'He was by Tom's first wife.'

She was called, unbelievably, Dolores.

'I see. Yes. I mentioned Morecambe a moment ago, didn't I?'

'Yes.'

'You know tall Miss Trimmer?'

'Yes.'

'She had twin sisters drowned there in 1912, so she told me.'

'Drowned?'

'Drowned.'

'Both at once?'

'Oh, yes. You don't make the same mistake twice, do you?'

She smiled, Mrs Capes was pleased to see.

Mrs Gadny asked, 'Aren't you going to turn the page?'

'Yes. Yes. My mind went for a minute – I was picturing those girls.' She laughed. 'Now what have we? Relations. Uncle Sam, Uncle Matthew, Uncle Bertie, Auntie Mary, Auntie Ruth.' Another page. 'More relations. That one there with the eyes

49

is Cousin Charlie. He ended up in Africa. Nothing more was heard.'

'Who's a good girl? Who's finished her junket?'

'He could have been eaten, for all anybody knew. Stewed in a pot.'

When did Miss Burns sleep?

'He had enough meat on him.'

At every hour of the day she sat upright, staring.

'My wedding.'

Wouldn't a meal have made her sleepy?

'My wedding, Faith.'

'Oh?'

'My wedding. Don't I look fetching?'

'You do.'

'I was thirty.'

'Thirty.'

'He was a fair bit older. Harry Capes. Handsome Harry.' She laughed, winked. 'Oh, he *was* too. And I loved him. At the time.' She paused. 'It was on a Sunday, it was the June of 1921; he'd been in the war, he'd come out of it in one piece.'

Tom had a scar to show.

'The church was St Peter's, near to the Lotbury Road. It was a beautiful wedding, Faith. And there was a nice reception, I remember. We went to Southsea for a week's honeymoon.'

'Did you?'

'Yes. Take the book, dear. You'll see the photos better.'

The photographs were black and white.

'There's two more pages of them – the wedding ones.'

Several faces.

'The woman with the eye-patch is his mother. Harry's. Dog clawed her right eye so she lost it. I called her "Nelson" once when I lost patience with her. She never did forgive me.'

'Oh?'

'I can't say I was happy with Harry.' She waited for a response. 'Because I wasn't.'

'There we are: all cosily tucked in.'

'He had a lot of nature in him, dear. Too much for me. He wore me out. And a few others.'

The laugh.

'It was that and the drink that killed him. Brought on his heart.'

She was looking at the wall.

'Why you staring, Faith?'

'Am I? Oh, dear.'

She had a book in her hands. The rash under her rib had begun to irritate: the night must be coming on.

'He was a child,' said Mrs Capes.

'Who?'

'Harry.'

'Harry. Yes. Your husband.'

'Sleep well, Mrs Hibbs.'

'He had to have everything his own way. It was always Harry first with him. I've never known a person as selfish as he was. And crafty! When it came to getting money for his drink, he was as crafty as a pox doctor's clerk.'

'As *what*?'

'"Crafty as a pox doctor's clerk." It was one of my mother's expressions. You never heard it before?'

'No. Never.'

'Have I shocked you?'

'No.'

'I thought – the look on your face—'

'No, I wasn't shocked. Not at all.'

'Night night. God bless.'

'Hark at her.'

'God bless.'

'My mother had so many expressions, she could have made a book of them. I only recall a few.'

Small mercies.

'Miss Burns, Miss Burns – it's time to close your eyes.'

Close? Eyes?

'Do you want to see the rest?'

'Yes.'

'Miss Burns, dear – lie back.'

'The rest are mostly of Barry. Harry and Barry – isn't it ridiculous?' She laughed. 'Barry was my boy, my son.'

'Was he?'

'Come along now. Slowly does it,' Nurse Trembath advised Miss Burns.

'We were very close. He doted on me.'

'You've had a long day.'

Staring.

'He hated his father. Not just disliked – really hated. Harry once took a strap to his backside, well nigh murdered him.

The boy never forgave... Every year, I had photos done of him... At one, at two, three, four, that's him at five... They don't show how beautiful he was—'

'Beautiful? A boy beautiful?'

'Why not?' A laugh that verged on a cough. 'He had fair hair, Faith, curly, and the palest blue eyes. And long lashes like a girl's. Everyone loved him. People, all kinds of different people, would turn in the street to look at him. And he was lovely, when he was older, sixteen and on, stripped down to his trunks – not a hair on him, skin like silk. He posed for painters.'

'Did he?'

'Yes. He took me one day to some picture gallery or other to see a painting of him. We went, and we looked and we couldn't see anything that bore a resemblance. Then we found it. It was called "The Young Warrior" and all it was was rows of black and white dots. Not a bit like Barry. He'd stood for a week in his buff in some freezing barn and he ended up as dots. The painter was famous, too, which surprised me.'

'Time for sleep.'

She would see Miss Burns sleep.

'We were more friends than mother and son. We kept Harry out of our lives, right out. He got in rages when he caught us laughing together. He knew we had no need of him.'

'Sweet dreams.'

'Turn the page, Faith dear... What do you see?'

'Ballet dancers.'

'The man in the photos is Barry.'

53

A Nancy. It was plain.

'He was a ballet dancer?'

'That's right.'

'I like a nice ballet.'

'I saved every penny to have him trained.'

'God bless.'

'He did very well. Went all over the world. Danced before royalty.'

'Where is he now?'

'Dead.'

'Dead?'

'Yes.'

'He must have been young.'

'Thirty-five.'

Her head was on the pillow, but her eyes were open. 'Thirty-five,' Mrs Capes repeated. She had to be sure Mrs Gadny had heard.

The nurse was coming towards them.

'Why aren't you ladies watching the television? It's a hospital play on tonight.'

'We're having a photo session, Nurse Trembath. Exchanging our memories. Just the two of us.'

'That *is* a good idea.'

'I've been tiring Faith with my stories. Haven't I, Faith? Still, it's her turn now. Let's look at yours, Faith.'

Faith, Faith.

'Can I stay and see?'

'Can she, Faith?'

'Yes.'

'I'll fetch a chair.'

She was soon back with a stool. She seated herself and announced that she was ready.

'Let battle commence.' Mrs Capes slammed her book shut.

Any photograph. This one:

'This is my husband. My Tom.'

'He's a charmer. He's a fine-looking man.' The nurse was struck. She went for a man with a scar.

'Oh, yes. He is. He is.'

Anything. This:

'This is my daughter. My Celia.'

'What a pretty creature!' said the nurse. Mrs Capes agreed.

'The day she got confirmed.'

'Very sweet.'

'And very pretty.'

This, this:

'This is my Tom again.'

'Upright, isn't he? Very upright.'

'Oh, yes. He is. He is.'

'A really handsome man.'

Celia at the zoo; at Greenwich.

Tom in uniform. Tom, with his pipe and what must have been his Bible, caught in a group in Flanders somewhere.

Another. Another.

They were like lead in her hands. She dropped a photo of Tom or Celia or herself or perhaps Mrs Barber or her Rose; she let it fall.

Miss Burns was awake.

'Pass us another one, Faith.'

'Yes, do.'

'Faith, dear, pass us another.'

It was so simple. It was the ideal solution. Smiling, she took a handful of photographs from the pile and proceeded to tear them neatly into strips.

'Faith—'

'Faith!' Mrs Gadny said, still smiling.

'Mrs Gadny!'

They were done for.

'Mrs Gadny!'

'What you doing?'

Wasn't it clear?

'Mrs Gadny, think what you're doing—'

'Stop it, Faith—'

'No!'

'Nurse, we must stop her.'

Hands.

Mrs Gadny screamed 'Don't touch me!' She was delighted she could sound so ferocious. 'Don't touch!'

They let her go.

'Mrs Gadny—'

'Your photos—'

'I don't need them. What use are they?'

'Reminders—'

'Souvenirs—'

'To stir memories—'

'I don't need them.' She added, serenely: 'I have their faces in my head. I have no use for photographs.'

'Do you remember what I said that day?... Oh dear, the rain's come on... Do you remember? I said if you have problems, you must bring them to me. We're all friends at the Jerusalem: we share our troubles. You tell me yours, Mrs Gadny – Faith, rather – you take your time and tell me.'

Matron smiled, shut the smile off quickly.

Mrs Gadny wondered why this woman should imagine she had problems. She felt happy, she had slept well. And she had nothing to say.

'Did your visitors bring bad news on Sunday?'

'No.'

'More like a monsoon than a storm, isn't it?'

There was thunder and lightning.

'Now, Faith' – she seemed to gulp as she spoke the name – 'relax yourself. Take a deep, deep breath and—'

'Nothing's the matter, Matron.'

And that's final.

'But there *must* be something.'

Would there be tea and biscuits? Or perhaps morning coffee? It was after eleven. A slice of layer cake would be appreciated.

Thunder and lightning.

'I hate to contradict you, dear, but there must be. Why should you tear up your photographs?'

The patterns the rain made on the window-panes. There was one that was like a face.

'You keep them for years and then you suddenly destroy them. Why?'

'I don't need them any more—'

'To remind you of—'

The dead.

'I don't need them.'

'You don't?'

'No. Not at all.'

I must be patient, Matron thought. I shall find the reason in time. This poor Mrs Gadny, such a gentle, remote creature; so obviously accustomed to quietness, politeness—

'If there is something wrong, I hope you realize that it does no good to keep it bottled up inside. When Nurse Trembath told me what you'd done, I was surprised I admit. It didn't seem *sensible*.'

'There's nothing the matter, Matron.'

'As you say.'

'Nothing at all.'

Nothing. Nothing.

'Then I shan't pursue the subject.'

—and she appeared to have some taste in clothes. She wore a plain dress, clearly not expensive, and a rope of imitation pearls, but she looked presentable. Each day saw a different outfit: she had a smart blue suit, a grey sweater and skirt, a pretty orange print. Her hands, though – they were the wonder: Matron had heard from the stepson about her years of service for the Honourable Somebody-or-Other, of how brightly she polished and how frequently scrubbed her small home. After such a life her hands should be swollen, should be the red of meat. But Mrs Gadny's hands were small and as fine and white as ivory. Matron remembered 'Ivory hands' from some song.

'Do you feel more settled?'

'Yes.'

'Have you any complaints?'

'No. No, Matron.'

'That's good.'

The face on the window had the sun behind it.

'The storm's soon over.'

'Yes.'

Then, to end the silence, Matron rose.

'Eat up all your lunch, won't you?'

The smile, it was more like a tic – it happened so suddenly.

Mrs Gadny lingered a moment in the chair. Perhaps Matron would remember tea or coffee.

'That's all, my dear.'

Mrs Gadny got up slowly.

Outside, in the corridor with the green-and-white tiles on the walls, she stood for a moment and smiled. It was probably just as well that tea had not been served – she might have been forced to listen to more tales about Lord Whatsit.

The one, she thought, responsible for this place.

*

It was cooler everywhere, especially in the dining-hall. A hot meal could be tackled better.

'Where's your friend, Louise?' Miss Trimmer was intrigued by the vacant seat.

'Which friend could you mean, Edith?'

'I thought there *was* only one. Why – Faith.'

'I've no idea where she is.'

'No idea? You do surprise me. I thought you two had become so close you couldn't bear to be parted.'

Louise Capes had been alone all morning.

'You thought wrong, didn't you, Edith?'

Louise, Edith; Edith, Louise – no one had ever heard these two be so polite.

'She's in with Matron,' Mrs Affery said.

'Is she? Is she now? What's she done, Louise?'

'You *are* full of questions, aren't you? You don't usually speak to me, dear – not even to ask the time of day. It's not your custom.'

'She done something? Said something?' Miss Trimmer persisted.

'It's a marvel to me you don't know already. Your wits must be failing you. It isn't like you not to know what's up.'

One of Mrs Crane's pieces of roast lamb had some blood in it.

'It must be something dreadful, something really shocking, for you not to tell us—'

'It's worrying you, Edith—'

'What could *she* have done that's dreadful? She smuggle a man in?' Miss Trimmer waited for the laughter to subside.

'I wouldn't put it past her. These la-di-da ones, you know, are usually the first to offer their crumpets.'

Mrs Gross said 'Your talk!'

'Made you blush, have I, Nell?'

'Blush? Me! Me blush?'

'You went red.' Miss Trimmer was not to be distracted. 'Come on, Louise, tell me.'

'What's there to tell?'

'If anyone knows what it is, you do.'

Mrs Gross asked Mrs Capes would she put Miss Trimmer out of her misery?

'Misery, Mrs Gross? She's smiling all over her chops.'

'That's only a front. That's show.'

'I noticed she's lost her appetite. She hasn't had a single bite of her dinner.'

Her back was firmly against the door. She stared into the water.

'Celia, love.'

How swiftly things changed. Hadn't she been happy an hour ago? There'd been a lovely storm.

'Tom, love.'

Steam had been rising from the grass; she'd opened a window, inhaled the clean air.

'Celia, love.'

*

Miss Trimmer said, 'There's St Mary's striking one. She's an hour late. She and Matron must be having a lot to talk about.'

'She can't still be in there—'

'What time she go in, Maggy?'

'Who? Who go in?'

'Mrs Gadny, Maggy. Into Matron's office, Maggy.'

'Hours ago. Half-past eleven.'

Mrs Temple could see Matron and Nurse Trembath walking together. 'I think you'd better send out a search-party, Nurse. It looks as though Mrs Gadny's got lost.'

'Half-past eleven she went in. I was on my way to the lav and I passed her as she opened Matron's door.'

Mrs Capes cried suddenly: 'Nurse! Nurse!' She sounded like someone being attacked in a play.

'What is it?' asked Nurse Barrow.

'Mrs Gadny—'

Her mouth remained open.

'Yes?'

'Well, I think – the reason she's late—' Her face was white; a hand shook. 'She may be in the toilets – she may have gone there—'

'What's the matter with you?'

'Go and look for her, Nurse.' She paused before adding 'Please.'

They watched Nurse Barrow hurry out. She was a funny sight with her thin legs and great feet. She had three grey hairs sprouting from a wart on her chin. And her step was unmistakable – they could tell it was her two corridors away.

Miss Trimmer kept her eyes on Mrs Capes. 'You don't think… what Belle did?'

'I don't think I think anything—'

She must have been thinking something. Whenever Capes wiped her smile off was the time to worry.

'Not her,' said Miss Trimmer. She added, decisively: 'Not her.'

'No locks,' Mrs Affery reminded them. 'They took the locks.'

'That's right.'

'Yes. They took the locks.'

'But she has been gone an hour.'

'Not her.' Miss Trimmer was angry – all this concern for that miserable Mrs Gadny; she was afraid she'd shown some herself when she'd asked if the woman had done what Belle had done. As if Mrs Gadny would do anything! She was far too occupied with her own silly troubles, hoarding them like a miser. That tiny whining voice. The way her head went down when she was in company.

And now no one was speaking.

'Why we all struck dumb?' Miss Trimmer wanted to know. 'I shall eat what's left of my blancmange.'

They listened as she ate.

Sure enough, she was still alive. Mrs Capes looked noticeably relieved as Mrs Gadny came into the hall hand in hand with Nurse Barrow. Miss Trimmer smiled: she had had no doubts on the matter. The nurse spoke in a loud, bright voice: 'Who forgot her lunch? Mrs Gadny forgot all about her lunch.'

'Yes. I did.'

The nurse, who always walked quickly, had been slowed down to funeral pace.

'I've kept your food under a hot plate. Shoulder of lamb, dear.'

'Yes... That sounds nice.'

'Peas and new potatoes. Take your place, Mrs Gadny, and I'll bring it to you. The other ladies have finished. They're all waiting for their cups of tea.'

Mrs Gadny took her place.

'Good afternoon, Faith.' Mrs Capes tried to keep her voice steady.

'Good afternoon.'

Mrs Capes decided she would stay quiet. She was having one of her rare upsets. It usually took her an hour or more to shake them off.

Mrs Gadny's head was down.

'Tasty piece of lamb today,' said Mrs Gross.

'Is it?'

'We all agreed.'

She knew they were staring at her: eyes in front, eyes on either side and the nurse's eyes behind.

'I want to see that plate empty, Mrs Gadny.'

The food to deal with.

She heard Mrs Crane ask Mrs Temple to pass the mint sauce.

*

It was close in the ward. The women were restless; sheets were in disarray.

Mrs Affery fought with her bedclothes. Mrs Gadny had watched her changing shape in the half-light: now a hump, now jerking up and down like a snake. Once her hands darted into the air, became fists that banged and banged against a door or perhaps somebody's chest.

Mrs Temple had emptied herself twice without making use of the screen.

A letter would make some of the time pass. The light was strong enough. Thinking a little of what to tell Mrs Barber would make her deaf to the moaning that was coming from Mrs Affery and to the birds when they started. A blackbird had begun.

'Dear Mrs Barber,' she wrote, 'you are a very wicked woman.' She smiled.

Why do I call you that. I call you wicked because you have still not written to me your old friend and neighbour has watched every post in the hope of hearing from you.

Mrs Hibbs – whose head dangled, whose mouth was open – had received a letter. Nurse Trembath, who had read it to her, said it was written on scented paper.

She saw Mrs Affery beating the air. She wrote quickly, in her firmest hand:

I wish I was in Cornwall. I wish I was a thousand miles from this place. To make it worse the weather has broken and it has rained fit enough to drown a regiment and all this night it has been hot that humid heat.

A black gap. Her mouth open. A black gap.

It is hard for me to stay on the cheerful side—

The moan. The gap wider now. A hole.

—words from you would help. I dont mean that as flattery you know me I was never the KIND WHO FAWNS. But to hear from you even a note even a card would be a breath of fresh air as they say.

Keep writing—

The last time I wrote to you it was to say that THEY were coming to see me. Well dear they *did* come poking their noses about asking all manner of things. They asked me SHE asked rather if I was eating as if I would stop because I wasnt living with them I could see her meaning. Did I wash she asked me. Did I wash. You will be pleased to hear that I gave her a few words. I said in no uncertain terms that they had got rid of me like trash waste I said.

The moan again.

You know all my photos Mrs Barber the ones I kept all those years in that shoebox. I give you one guess what I have done with them.

She waited for Mrs Barber to answer her. 'What did I do with them?' she heard herself ask.

She wrote:

I give you one guess what I have done with them. I tore them up. Yes I tore them up the night after Henry and her had been. In front of one of the Nurses and the woman I told you about the one called Capes (or K) I do beleive they thought I was mad.

The moan louder. Keep on—

How many more times must I ask you to write to me I wont send you a really long letter until you do. Anyway my dear this is where I shall sign off. Hoping you are in good health and the family your friend

F. E. GADNY (MRS)

The creature was awake.

'Oh. Oh. Oh dear, dear, dear. Dear me.'

Mrs Gadny rested her letter on the locker's top.

'Oh dear.'

The tall Miss Trimmer opened and closed an eye.

The creature sat up, beads of sweat streaming down her

face. 'Dear, dear.' She arranged her tippet about her shoulders. 'Dear, dear.'

Mrs Gadny was forced to scratch. It was most undignified but it had to be done.

Mrs Affery called across: 'Are you awake?'

She had her eyes open; she was scratching. 'Yes.'

Mrs Gadny saw the creature's legs make for the floor. They dangled a moment, bluey-white, then descended. Her bumpy feet found their way into a pair of shoes.

Now, bent over, feet on tip-toe, she was coming nearer.

'You awake?' The creature's lips moistened. 'You awake?'

'Yes.'

'I had one of my dreams. It was terrible.'

She applied the bottom of her grey nightdress to her face, dabbed at the sweat. 'I'm soaked.' Mrs Gadny could not turn her eyes away from the sight of Mrs Affery's white belly and the hairs beneath it. Doctor Gettrup said: We want to see that you're fit in every department.

'A man with a knife in his hand was after me.'

'Was he?'

'Yes.'

Mrs Affery sat on the bed by Mrs Gadny's feet.

'He had staring eyes.'

'Had he?'

'Yes.' She swallowed some air. 'His hair was black as pitch.'

Mrs Gadny was more polite than curious when she asked Mrs Affery who he was.

'There you have me. But he knew who I was. He came round

this corner quiet as a cat and he said "I've come for you, Maggy."
He had a posh voice; gold on his teeth.'

'Really?'

'Really and truly. He laughed at me and let me go and then
I ran. I ran and ran. This was the funny part – I was running
and he was walking but he was always just behind me. "I'm
here, Maggy," he was saying. Then I lost my breath, I was in
this alley – it was a real one, it was by Itchy Common, near
where I lived as a girl – and he come up close and he laughed.
I tried to kick him in the conkers but I missed.'

A thin length of spit was secured to her lower lip. It shook
in the light. Mrs Gadny would not have been surprised to see
a spider make use of it. Mrs Affery demolished it with the back
of her hand.

'Then what do you think?'

'What?'

'His face changed and there was my husband. Which was
when I woke.'

'You're shaking.'

'I know I am. Wouldn't you be?'

'Yes.'

'I thought he was the Ripper. He was doing his murders the
year I was born. I used to dream about him when I was young.
My mother'd say to me "If you don't behave yourself I'll set the
Ripper on to you." That's what she'd say.'

'Would she?'

'Or he might've been Spring-heeled Jack.'

Mrs Affery stood up. She coughed. Spit came from the side

of her mouth, hung like a chain. She sucked it back and said, 'Whoever he was, he give me a turn.'

'Did he?'

'Can't you see?'

'Yes.'

'The eyes on him. And then to find he was my Dan!'

The mouth was above her: opening, closing; the black gap, the hole. She prayed there would be no more spit. She got a mouthful of tippet instead. She wanted to scream; she managed a cough. It rid her of the offending object. Then Mrs Affery yanked it away.

'Dan and me fought like thieves.'

Did you, did you? 'Did you?'

Now she talked of operations. The woman was crazy. One minute she was saying about her and her Dan fighting like thieves, the next she was carrying on about operations. The belly was displayed again and a scar carefully fingered.

'This hospital's in Lambeth, where they done it. They have a machine there, it's the only one of its kind; just for stomachs. People come from all over the world to take advantage. All over the world... Dulwich – everywhere.'

She'd felt empty afterwards, she said; they had taken out the lot.

Doctor Gettrup said she had good eyes.

'Sh! Sh!'

Mrs Affery, turning, saw Miss Trimmer with one eye open. 'Would be her, wouldn't it?'

Doctor Gettrup was amazed that most of her teeth were real.

'She'll never let me hear the end of it.'

Mrs Gadny smiled. Mrs Affery thought: She has a kind face.

Mrs Affery leaned over her again. 'Did I *wake you* up?'

'No.'

'You sure?'

'Yes.'

'I'd hate to feel—'

'I can't sleep in this weather.'

And never could.

'I'd hate to think—'

'I can't sleep when it's hot.'

Or facing you, you creature, you – 'Sh! Sh!'

'It's *her*. "Sh!" yourself.'

Other women stirred.

'I'll carry my bones back with me to bed, dear.'

Mrs Affery smiled down at her. Anywhere else, appearing suddenly in a street for instance, Mrs Gadny would have felt happy at the sight of those wet lips, that ridiculous, dirty tippet: Mrs Affery could have been a clown. But not in here.

Mrs Affery feared for the Trimmer wrath to come. She whispered, 'It was nice talking.' She honoured Mrs Gadny with her widest smile.

'"Celia, Celia," she was saying, so Nurse Barrow said. The other day when she found her.' Mrs Gross stood close to her friend and spoke very quietly.

Miss Trimmer asked in her normal voice, 'Who's Celia when she's out?'

Mrs Gross looked at the wash-room door before she replied. 'Her daughter. Dead now.'

'No use calling for her then, is it? She won't hear where she is.'

'What a remark to make!'

'Why call for a dead person? That's all I'm saying. Unless she's one of those stupid moos who turn the lights out and look into crystal balls. What they called?'

'They're called spiritualists, Edie, and they don't look into crystal balls neither. Fortune-tellers do that. No, a spiritualist sits round a table with a lot of people and gets the dead to send messages to them.'

'Messages?'

'Yes. Messages of love and such. Old Mr Gamfield who lived next door to me, he got a message through a spiritualist. It was from his wife – she was a Mabel – and she told him not to marry again as he'd planned to do. He didn't heed her warning. He got married to some girl half his age and he died a week after the wedding.'

'Poor sod. He wear it out?' Miss Trimmer laughed.

'You can laugh.'

'Your face, Nell – so solemn you are.'

'What's funny about what I said?'

'Nothing, Nell.'

'What caused you to laugh?'

'That tripe about the messages. That eye-wash.'

'It's not tripe or eye-wash. You don't understand it. You only see things that are stuck in front of you.'

'Safer, Nell. Much safer. Anyway, you were telling me what Nurse Barrow said—'

'No more to tell. All Mrs Gadny was doing was standing in the second toilet from the end calling out her daughter's name. Not even calling out, now I think of it – just saying.'

'She needs to be put away.'

'Why does she?'

'I wouldn't say calling out names in the lavatory was normal.'

'Only a phase she's going through. You *do* do odd things when you feel lonely.'

'Do you?'

'You know you do, Edith.'

Miss Trimmer reminded Mrs Gross that they had come here to wash. She waited for the water to warm before she removed her vest. 'It was her and that bloody Maggy woke me up with their bloody chatter this morning. What with *her* and Alice Temple perched on the jerry half the night, a person gets no peace at all.'

The earth outside smelled so clean, it was easy to forget the graves. She stood at the window; inhaled. Days ago, after a similar storm, she had done the same. She remembered that shortly afterwards she had gone to the lavatory, chosen the cleanest cubicle, remained there: Celia's cough had come distinctly. Today she would be cheerful. She would do her best to stay perky, bright.

She ate all her porridge at breakfast; licked her spoon clean. She would go to the main hall. Mrs Barber's letter would be very long and friendly.

The card had a picture of the Dome at Brighton. 'Dear – It has rained and rained. Edna and Young Michael very upset. Henry eat prawns on Tuesday – his stomach very bad since. I have read 3 romances and eat to many chocolates. Hope alls well. All our love Thelma.'

She would try to be bright.

Matron always seemed to make her speeches on steak-and-kidney days. She begged the ladies to please continue eating while she spoke.

'You will be very happy to learn that we have at last decided upon the date for our annual outing. It will take place on the last Sunday of the month – the twenty-ninth of July.'

'Where we going, Matron?'

'Show a little patience, Mrs Crane.' She gave a smile to soften the reprimand. 'The unanimous decision this year is that we should visit Southend.'

The information set them murmuring. Matron heard Miss Trimmer say something about winkles and cockles.

'The coach will arrive at the main gate at eight a.m. We shall have a nice long day at the seaside.'

More murmurs.

'There is one other matter I have to mention. On August the third Mrs Hibbs will be ninety years old. It has been suggested to me that we hold a small birthday party and naturally I welcomed the idea most enthusiastically. Owing to Mrs Hibbs's disability, the party will take place in the ward. There will be a cake with nine candles – one for every decade of her life.'

The threat of rain had driven the women into the Home: some were in the dining-hall, some in the lounge.

Mrs Gadny sat on a bench. She would try to keep her mind empty – it was the sensible policy.

But here was Mrs Capes and her voice saying 'Smile.'

Smile!

Mrs Capes had sighted her from the corridor window, had seen she was alone, out in the cold – it was much cooler after that humid night, wasn't it? 'I felt so sticky in my bed, especially my legs – they *would* keep getting stuck together. Every time I parted them, they made a funny noise. It reminded me of someone letting the air out of a balloon.' She laughed. 'I think the summer's gone, Faith.'

'Do you?'

'No proper sunshine for days.'

'Oh?'

'You must have noticed.' Mrs Capes looked at Mrs Gadny. 'May I sit with you, dear?'

'Yes.'

'Yes?'

'Yes.'

'We haven't talked for days, have we? I've missed our chats. We must stop being polite and start being friends again.'

'Yes?'

'This bench is damp.'

'Then don't sit on it,' Mrs Gadny said.

'I've suffered worse.' She sat on the very edge of the bench. 'Far worse.' She laughed. 'Oh far, far worse.'

They sat in silence.

'Dear—', Mrs Capes began. Mrs Gadny stared ahead. 'Dear—'

Mrs Gadny was having one of her staring fits. This would rouse her: 'Are you feeling better, dear?'

'Better?'

'The state you were in last Monday night. I put it down to your son—'

'Stepson.'

'—your stepson coming to see you. And his wife.'

'They came on Sunday—'

'Still—'

'What state?'

'Showing your temper, dear. Tearing up your photos. And – I hate to remind you – you shouted at me.'

At last Mrs Gadny smiled. 'Not only you. The nurse as well.'

'The nurse as well.'

Mrs Gadny's smile spread. 'The nurse as well,' she said, starting to laugh.

A most peculiar laugh, Mrs Capes considered; not one you could share in.

The noise ended.

'I can't say I find Southend a suitable choice for our outing,' Mrs Capes said. 'I find Southend so common. I would have preferred Bournemouth, say, or Morecambe: where the people are pleasanter. Last year it was Brighton we went to.'

Henry's stomach's bad; Thelma says it's raining and raining – there's some justice in the world.

'You gave me such a fright on Tuesday.'

'Fright?'

'When you got lost—'

'Lost?'

'When you disappeared—'

'Disappeared?'

Lord. 'When you were in the toilet, dear.'

'Why shouldn't I go to the toilet? Everyone has to.'

'Yes, Faith, yes.'

'Why should that give you a fright?'

'It's difficult to say without offending.'

'What is?'

'Well, dear. Well…'

'Well?'

'I thought – what I told you about Belle Waters—'

Silence.

'I shan't hang myself,' Mrs Gadny said.

'For a minute on Tuesday my stomach turned right over.'

'As if I'd do that!'

The thought had never occurred.

'It was Maggy Affery saying she'd been to the lav – she never says "toilet". It was her saying that set my mind off. I remembered telling you about Belle, what she'd done, and then it struck me you might've—'

'As if I would! As if I'd do that!'

'I had this horrible picture of you, you hung limp, and as I say, my stomach went straight to my mouth.'

She had stared into the water.

'"It was me", I thought to myself, "who put the idea into her head."'

'As if I'd ever do that!'

'Though, in my heart of hearts, I knew you wouldn't. It was only for a minute, Faith, I had the thought.'

'I'd never. Never.'

'I know. It was the state you were in.'

'What state?'

'Last Monday.'

'No state.'

'No.' What use was it, arguing? 'No.'

A large raindrop fell on to the bench between them. 'Picture me doing *that*.'

'I know. It's ridiculous. Forgive me mentioning—'

'The very thought.'

A black cloud covered the sun.

'Concerned for me, were you?' Mrs Gadny asked. 'Need you ask, dear?'

'Thank you for being concerned.'

Rain was a certainty now. They watched more drops des-
cend. The birds that had been in the grass hurried to the trees.

'In spite of my cheerful nature, I always expect the worst.
You can't believe that, can you, looking at me?' No response.
'It's true. It's the way I am.'

'Is it?'

'It is. Oh, yes. I put a smile on things because I think it best.'
Mrs Nutley said: I put a smile on things. Matron said: Smile.
Mrs Capes went on: 'But I wouldn't say I don't worry—'

'Because you do.'

'Because I do. One story I'll tell you—'

Her stories. 'Story?'

'Yes, dear. It's what you'd call unusual. It'll show you what I
mean about expecting the worst. It's about my Barry.'

'Is it?'

'Yes. Do you know, I sensed that he'd died a whole day
before I found out for certain. A whole day before! Isn't that
strange, Faith? I was in a butcher's one Friday, the man was
cutting me off a piece of pork, a piece off the leg and as I was
watching him I saw Barry's face in front of me. Then the
butcher asked if I'd had a turn and I said "No, I'm all right"
and I went home. I brooded on it. On the Saturday the police
called. I told them I knew what had happened.'

She had told the story before because of its unusual nature.
Several people had heard it; some had said she must have
psychic powers. The strangeness of it had struck her months
later, the first time she visited Madame Merle.

I was in a quandary after Barry's death, Mrs Capes said

to herself. I went to Madame Merle on Mrs Forbes's advice. I went to her to get a message from Barry. I went to her for comfort.

Mrs Capes, after mulling the subject over, decided not to tell Mrs Gadny about Madame Merle. She would keep *her* to herself. She would never tell the other ladies (ladies!) either: they would disbelieve her anyway, disbelieving cusses.

Mrs Gadny was glad that Mrs Capes had gone quiet.

Comfort, she remembered, was what she'd needed. That was a terrible time, that March through to September. Thank God it'd been lived through! Barry's dying, first – he was stuck there on the kitchen floor for four whole days before they discovered him. And all because of that bloody George: bloody Hungarian, bloody foreigner. With eyes as shifty as his, what could you expect? She'd never told anyone about *him*: she was almost ashamed (perhaps *ashamed* was too strong) of her Barry, who followed his mother in his commonsense (and was romantic as well, just like her) – she was almost ashamed of him taking that horror seriously. If only she had warned him… They were always frank with one another, more like friends than mother and son. She remembered Barry telling her about his leanings. (He used to put a voice on when he said the word 'leanings' – very plummy, like a clergyman. 'Come up and see my leanings,' he used to say.) Anyhow, that time he told her about himself: he'd tried, he said, doing it with a girl. Only once. And once was more than enough, thank you. Even then he'd had to down a half-bottle of Scotch to give him the courage. He kissed and cuddled with the girl and then he took her to bed.

The poor little love couldn't manage more than half-mast, not *that* after a while. So from that night it was definitely boys for Barry Capes. Oh, she laughed and laughed when he told her! The expression he put on! He was a born mimic.

Mrs Gadny hoped Mrs Capes wouldn't spoil the peace with her chatter.

He left her a little money. He'd squandered most of it on bloody George: clothes, clothes, more clothes. She thought of the presents he used to send *her*: lovely dark Floris chocolates, lovely scents; she still had a bottle in her locker, a French one, it smelt a bit like that stuff they shake about in churches. She'd give Faith a drop if they became friends again. It helped you through the day, smelling nice – especially in a place like the Jerusalem.

If Mrs Capes stayed silent, she could have her doze.

Lots of his dancer friends turned out for his funeral. One hymn was sung. And Serge – he was Welsh, was Serge – made a speech about Barry: what a pleasure it had been, teaching him; how he might have scaled great heights. Everyone was sorry for her. She managed little smiles for Barry's special friends – you had to cling on to your dignity on such occasions. She was proud of the way she behaved that day – it was a test of her character, it required strength of mind.

Mrs Gadny closed her eyes.

Days later, she recalled, she began to go to pieces. She'd known what was happening to her; hadn't been able to stop it… The drinking, for example. She sat, night after night, on her stool in the saloon of the Palace Arms, knocking back the gins. Some nights she staggered home. One night – it humiliated her to think of it – she collapsed in the bar. 'You're not the first to suffer a loss,' a woman she'd never been able to put a name to said to her. What a memory to drag up. The shame… And the terrible months that followed. If the April was bad, the May was worse. She'd hated the hot days most: it was wicked that Barry, who loved the sun, should not be living to enjoy it. Then, one evening in the June, she saw George's face on the pub television. He was playing the part of a waiter. When the play was over, she rang the B.B.C. and asked a snotty-sounding woman if her boss made a habit of employing refugees who were nothing better than money-grubbing pansies. She smiled at the recollection.

Mrs Forbes it was who brought her to her senses. Not only was she a wonderful person to work for, she was a true friend. All through those months she was never at a loss for a kind word. Several evenings Mrs Forbes asked her to stay on at the house to take a little dinner with her… Everything came to a head on a Sunday in the August. They ate a lavish dinner – prawns cooked in cream, roast duck with apples. Over coffee with a glass of vintage brandy Mrs Capes began to snivel. It took hold of her – sob, sob, sob. Mrs Forbes said 'Louise' – it was always 'Louise' – 'I know the answer to your problems.' Mrs Forbes went on to mention Madame Merle, what a brilliant woman she was. 'That woman has brought my husband to me, Louise. And *he* was buried in Africa.'

'Faith, dear—' Turning her head, Mrs Capes saw that Mrs Gadny had closed her eyes.

Madame Merle had this enormous house – great rooms, huge garden. The furniture shone. She had grey hair done up in black ribbon and the top row of her teeth was always covered in lipstick. She had a soft, faraway voice and a French accent.

'Faith—'

This was going to be more than a shower.

'Faith, dear. Wake up.'

'I'm not asleep.'

'We'd best go in.'

'Yes.'

Mrs Capes remembered the other clients at Madame Merle's: a Miss Carew in a dirty macintosh, a Colonel Weekes. He looked a rum old boy.

As they walked back to the Home, Mrs Capes took Mrs Gadny's hand, pressed it hard. She'd had three sessions with Madame Merle: at the last Barry had begged her to be happy and sensible again. That was enough for her. And anyway Mrs Forbes had died of a stroke – *she* couldn't afford to pay Madame Merle out of her own small amount. 'Thank you for all your help, Madame,' she'd said. 'You've changed my life.' 'That's what I live to hear, Mrs Capes,' were Madame's last words to her.

Mrs Forbes left her a pair of ear-rings and a gold watch.

When it was wet there was no escaping them. They were everywhere. At meals you could look at your food; the rest of the day was a hell on earth. You turned a corner and the creature's yellow face above the tippet was coming for you. If you went to the toilet very soon someone would suspect you of doing something and either bang on or open the door. In the lounge – that hateful word – they sat about or slept with their mouths open. And, if they had eaten too much, they made noises and sometimes smells.

If you sat on your bed you had to face the one called Burns. And there was Mrs Hibbs. You couldn't read a book or a paper just yet, you had too many thoughts that took your mind off.

When the sun was out a day here was a more bearable business. After breakfast, after mid-day dinner, after tea you could sit in the grounds. If Mrs Capes was about, you could sleep or pretend to. There were graves, yes, but there were trees, birds; the sky was above.

The rainy weather lasted a week. The sun appeared on a Wednesday. Mrs Gadny placed a newspaper on the bench to protect herself from the damp. She sat alone for more than an hour.

When she awoke, Mrs Capes was sitting beside her.

She wanted to say: I've seen enough of you.

'Hullo, dear.'

'Hullo.'

This past week she had listened to so much chatter, so many stories: Barry here, Barry there, bloody Barry everywhere. Mrs Gadny smiled.

'You look happy.'

'Yes.'

'I don't know why you do. Look at those clouds.'

Look, indeed. Look at them, gathering.

She could feel the weariness taking possession of her bones. She wondered if she was still capable of lifting her arms.

'Just look.'

Look!

Mrs Capes said you could never trust the English weather. Her son had taken her to Monte once.

'Leave me in peace, Mrs Capes.'

'You want me to sit quiet? I understand, dear. I know I chatter.' She laughed. 'I get so caught up in what I say, I don't—'

'Go away from me.'

Go away from her?

'Is that too much to ask of you? You upset me, Mrs Capes.'

'Upset?'

'Yes.'

'How could I? It was the furthest thing from my mind to upset you. Now how could I?'

'You do.'

'Oh, Faith,' Mrs Capes said. 'Oh, Faith,' she repeated, and gave her laugh. 'It's the weather turning's made you—'

'No, it's not—'

'—irritable.'

Mrs Capes sighed loudly. Then she yawned.

'Aren't you going?'

'Going?'

'I asked you to go.'

'I'm not here to answer your orders.' After a silence, Mrs Capes said: 'I am not here to answer *your* orders.'

'Leave me in peace.'

'I shall sit here if I choose. These grounds and these benches were put here for the benefit of all of us. I shall stay where I am.'

She was beginning to grow accustomed to Faith's little tantrums. They came and went. Hers was the type who always suffered afterwards. The poor woman was probably working out a way to apologize this very minute. Mrs Capes decided not to accept the first apology – a second would be much more heartfelt.

Minutes later, the rain started.

'Rain,' said Mrs Capes. 'Rain's starting.'

'I'm not blind, Mrs Capes.'

'We shall have to go in.' – She isn't blind, but you'd think she was deaf. – 'We shall have to go in.'

Mrs Capes stood in front of Mrs Gadny. 'Aren't you coming in?'

'No.'

'You must. The rain'll come on heavy.'

'Let it.'

'Let it! Now come along.'

'Go away.'

'As you choose. Catch your death, then.'

'Go away.'

'"Go away, go away." Listen to you. Like a child.'

'Go away.'

'Are you coming in?'

'Go away.' She spoke quietly. 'Go.'

'I will. I will go.'

But she remained where she was.

'I've seen enough of you. Oh go.'

'I will. I will go. Catch bloody pneumonia.' Mrs Capes paused, took a breath, shouted at the stupid woman who might have been a friend: 'Catch bloody pleurisy.'

Mrs Gadny's head was down in that irritating way.

'If you ask me, you're simple.'

'Go. Go.'

'"Go. Go. Go away. Go away."'

Mrs Capes turned her back on Mrs Gadny and made her way past the graves. Nearing the Home she stopped, thought a moment, swung round. She shouted again:

'If you ask me, you're simple. You've gone simple.'

She waited for a reply. Nothing. She walked briskly into the Home.

Oh, it was soft, it was warm.

There was a water-butt in the garden. Her father worked the handle for her while she washed. On summer mornings his chest was bare except for his braces.

She felt her head. Water was flattening her hair. The drops ran down her face, down her nose – she laughed to see one drop dangle on the tip. She lifted her face to the water as she did when a girl. She closed her eyes.

A voice.

'You silly woman, Mrs Gadny. Come along.'

The nurse with the name. Nurse Barrow stood by her.

'Once you're dry, it's into bed with you.'

Hands.

'Take her other arm.'

They were hoisting her up from the bench. The water wasn't water – it was rain.

'Come with us.'

She couldn't move.

'I can't move. I can't move.' Fear had come into her voice. 'I can't move!'

'Your legs might have gone to sleep,' Nurse Barrow suggested. 'You've been sat here for hours. Shake the left first.'

The weight.

'And the right.' Nurse Trembath had her right arm.

As she was led away, she began to cry.

'There. There.'

'There.'

'There.'

Some of the women were at the window.

Sipping her cocoa, which was still very hot, Mrs Capes said to Mrs Gross: 'I told her stories. Many a time I tried to make her laugh. You know how often I sat and talked with her. I studied her in all manner of ways.'

'Yes,' Mrs Gross nodded, 'you did.'

'I did, didn't I? No one can say I didn't.'

'No.'

Miss Trimmer wondered why Mrs Capes had ever bothered with her.

'Matron asked me to—'

'Did she? *Did she?*'

'It was more than that: I didn't speak to her just because of Matron. I felt sorry for her.'

'Of course you did,' said Mrs Gross. She challenged her friend to say otherwise.

'That's right.' Miss Trimmer spoke in a disbelieving voice.

'She seemed so shy, so on her guard. I remember what I felt like when I first came. And she looked such a quiet person, respectable—'

'Not like us, eh?'

'Don't put words into my mouth, Edith.'

'She loves doing that.'

Mrs Crane asked them to lower their voices. She wanted to hear what the parson on the screen had to say.

'I went out of my way to help her.'

'Yes.'

'Which is more than some I could name did. More than Trembath or Barrow.'

'Yes.'

'You saw today the gratitude I got!'

They'd seen.

Mrs Gross ventured the thought that Mrs Gadny might be sick in herself.

'Which is what I told her.'

'Did you?'

'Did you?'

'When I lost my temper. In the rain. I said to her "You're simple."'

'Dear, dear.'

'She'd hurt me, hadn't she? Without a thought for my feelings.' Mrs Capes spoke rapidly. '*And* after all I'd done. But, you see, I'm like that, Mrs Gross, I leave myself open. I put my trust in people and I end up getting hurt by them. It's one lesson I've never taken to heart. Someone could ask me for help this minute and I'd put myself out, regardless. I would.'

Mrs Gross and Miss Trimmer stayed silent.

My dear Mrs Barber. Still no word from you. Even so here is another letter from me I hope it finds you in good health.

It has been a bad day for me I can safely say dear Mrs Barber that I have never felt so alone as I did today in my whole life.

I did a mad thing Mrs Barber I sat out in the rain it was really pouring down Mrs Barber it was cats and dogs. I sat out on a bench in the rain and I was crying if you asked me why I am sure I could never be able to tell you the Nurses had to help me up because I wasnt able to move Mrs Barber. Then they took my dress off and they put me in a hot bath then they dried me. My back is still sore (and raw) from where the nurse was rubbing. Then they gave me hot bovril and aspirins. It is morning as I write.

That woman I wrote to you about Mrs Barber the one called Kapes I told her to go away from me today I told her to leave me in peace I said it to her straight. I had better break off Mrs Barber as Nurses will only tell me off for sitting up in bed when I should be tucked in from the cold (Its warm) I know you will write soon as you are a true friend pass on my regards to all the family.

Best wishes

FAITH.

P.S. I have put Faith as it is more friendly than always putting Mrs Gadny we have known each other over 20 years after all.

'Ah, Mrs Gadny – Faith – do sit down.'

She sat opposite Matron.

Nurse Barrow attempted to leave. 'Stay, Nurse,' Matron said.

Matron put her arms on the desk. 'You had a little upset with Mrs Capes, I hear.'

'I told her to leave me in peace.'

'In peace?'

'Yes. She kept talking.'

'She was being friendly.'

'I told her to go away. I said it to her straight.'

'I also hear that you sat out in the rain. What a foolish thing to do!'

Mrs Gadny stared ahead.

'You are wondering why I asked you here?' Mrs Gadny seemed to be watching a fly on the wall. 'Mrs Gadny—'

'Yes.'

'You are wondering why I asked you here?'

'Yes.'

'Well. This morning, Mrs Gadny, I received a letter. It is from a Miss Rose Barber.'

'From Rose?'

'Yes.'

'To *you?*'

'To me. I shall read it out to you.'

'I can read myself. And I can write and spell.'

'I prefer to read it out to you.'

'Is Rose a friend of yours?'

'No.'

How strange.

'Sit back in your chair.'

She tried to settle.

'This letter has been sent from an address in Cornwall.'

'Yes.'

'"Dear Madam", it begins, "I hope you will forgive me writing out of the blue, so to speak. I realize you are a busy woman so I will keep this letter on the short side. I am very worried about one of the ladies under your care. Her name is Faith Ethel Gadny and she was a friend of my mother's."'

'Mrs Barber.'

'Mrs Barber. Miss Barber continues, "I believe she has not

been long at your Home. Has she got over her daughter's passing yet? It must have been a blow – they were as close as people can be. I ask you because it looks to me like the only reason for what she has been doing."'

Doing?

Matron raised her voice. "'Some while ago I began to receive letters from Mrs Gadny."'

'Not to Rose. The letters weren't for Rose.'

'Let me finish reading. "They came to the above address with my mother's name on the envelopes. My mother has been dead for two years."'

'No.'

'She says "My mother has been dead for two years. Mrs Gadny was invited to the funeral. She could not get down for it as she had a back complaint at the time. Celia, her daughter, and she sent a beautiful wreath of lilies. We missed Mrs Gadny at the funeral because Mother and she had been warm friends. They were neighbours for all of twenty years. That is why I find it strange that she should have written these letters. They are written, Madam, as though my mother was still alive. They are all about the Jerusalem Home and her stepson and daughter and others besides. It is a sad business." Are you listening, Mrs Gadny?'

'I am.'

"'It is a sad business. I feel pity for her but there is nothing I can do. She must be made to see that my mother is dead and buried. And it is painful to me also to keep receiving such morbid things through the post. I am afraid I must leave the matter in your hands. Please send any news to the above. Yours in good faith, Rose Barber (Miss)."'

'Well! Well, well!'

'You heard it all?'

'I heard.'

'When did she die?'

'Who?'

'Mrs Barber. Your friend Mrs Barber.'

'She's alive. Not dead.'

Matron stood up. 'It is important that you understand. Mrs Barber is dead.'

'No.'

'And has been for two years.' She picked up the letter. '"My mother has been dead for two years."'

'I would have been told. Someone would have told me.'

'You were invited to the funeral.'

Mrs Gadny laughed.

'Why do you laugh, Faith?'

'The idea.'

'Idea?'

'Of the funeral. Only the dead have those.'

'But Mrs Barber *is* dead,' said Nurse Barrow.

'How do you know?'

'Her daughter. Her daughter says.'

'Her!'

That shut them up.

'How many letters have you written?' Matron asked.

'Let me see. Four. Four. One went off in the post this morning.'

'There must be no more.'

'Why not?'

'You heard what Miss Barber wrote to me.'

'Lies. She's a liar. She always was.'

'Consider her feelings, my dear.'

'The stories she told my Celia. The lies she used to tell.'

Nurse Perceval entered with her trolley. She brought a pot of coffee and a chocolate cake.

Matron sat down. 'Pour Mrs Gadny some coffee. Nurse.'

'I'd appreciate a slice of cake as well.'

'And give her a slice of cake as well.'

The coffee was strong, the cake on the hard side.

Matron might have been a navvy, the noise she made drinking.

'Would you like a room?' Matron asked.

'Room? Where?'

'Here. In the Jerusalem. All to yourself. A bed and a table and a view out of the window and flowers. A room on the top floor.'

'Why?'

'Won't it be nicer for you?'

'Yes… Why?'

'We came to a decision. Didn't we, Nurse Barrow? Nurse Perceval?'

'Yes, Matron' from the nurses.

'We decided you would be happier in your own room.'

'Why?'

'You don't enjoy company, do you? You prefer to keep to yourself. You don't need to be chattering all day, do you?' She whispered: 'The other ladies – they aren't your kind of people, are they?'

'No.'

'Would you like to see your room?'

'Yes.'

'Nurse Barrow will take you there. And see to your belongings... We shall bring you your meals on a tray.'

'Why?'

'Because we want you to have every comfort.'

'Why?'

'It's our job. Our duty.'

'Yes.'

Hands. Nurse Barrow's on her shoulders.

'Up you get, Mrs Gadny. Come along with me. Come along to your nice room.'

She would like another piece of cake—

'I shall pay you a visit, Faith, as soon as you're settled.' Matron smiled, shut the smile off quickly.

'Up the stairs we go.'

At the top of this flight, which was the third they'd climbed, they entered a corridor.

The tiles were green.

Nurse Barrow opened a door.

'Open, Sesame,' Mrs Gadny said. They laughed.

The room had white walls. A small window, she saw. A bed. A table. A chair. A bowl of chrysanthemums.

She sniffed the chrysanthemums. They were real.

'Very nice, isn't it?'

'Yes.'

'Cosy.'

On the wall that was just bricks painted over she noticed a picture. 'St John On The Island Of Patmos' were the words underneath it. In the country, years back, she'd had a picture of St Peter. It was mainly purple. Behind St Peter were clouds that looked like white steps leading to heaven.

'Try the bed… How is it?'

'It's too soft. I'm used to a hard bed. It *is* what I'm accustomed to.'

'Then we shall have to find another mattress. Come to the window, Mrs Gadny.'

They stood together, looking out.

'No graves here, Mrs Gadny. We're at the front of the building. Over there beyond the street's the common. You see the children playing?'

'Oh, yes. On the grass.'

'Don't you feel better already?'

'Yes. Yes.'

'Do you want to go anywhere?'

'Go?'

'To do the necessary?'

'No.'

'I shall see to your lunch. Stew today. And apple Charlotte. Why don't you sit in your chair?'

Mrs Gadny sat down.

'You stay there until I return.'

Mrs Gadny looked at St John on his island. She didn't hear Nurse Barrow turn the key in the lock.

Matron told them of her decision regarding Mrs Gadny. She smiled at them and left the hall.

'What a thing to happen!' said Mrs Crane.

'Who was the last to be put in there?' Miss Trimmer asked. 'Mad Annie Erskine, wasn't it?'

'Mad Annie Erskine, yes.' Several women spoke.

'Now it's the turn of Dotty Faith,' said Mrs Crane.

'Dotty Faith!'

'Dotty Faith!'

Mrs Gross was upset by the talk. 'There's a name to give her! The poor woman.'

Miss Trimmer didn't think she was bloody dotty. 'She's too crafty to be dotty. I see her tricks. Her mind works all right. How else would she get a room to herself?'

'She'll be treated,' said Mrs Affery. 'Doctors will come and look at her. As they did for Annie Erskine.'

The women returned to the meal.

'The noise you make eating, Mrs Crane,' Mrs Capes said across the table.

'Beg pardon, Madam.'

'Well!'

They continued to eat until Mrs O'Blath's laugh distracted them.

'Now what?' asked Miss Trimmer.

'What's tickled you, Peggy?' asked Mrs Crane.

'It's Maggy. She's got some gristle. Look at her chops going!'

Miss Trimmer said, 'Spit it out, Maggy. It'll only lodge in your throat.'

Mrs Affery spat the gristle into her bowl. Some stew splashed on to the table-cloth.

Mrs O'Blath couldn't contain herself. 'Do not spit, the notice says, Maggy. Signed, Matron.'

Mrs Affery wiped her mouth on a napkin; stared at Mrs O'Blath.

'Let her laugh,' she said to the other women. 'It's all she can do.'

Part Two

A pretty enough house, no doubt of that. A lot of care had been lavished on it. Each room had its own floral-patterned wallpaper, which was – she had to confess – an unusual touch.

'To think,' Thelma said, 'that in all these years you've never set foot before in Roselea.'

'It *is* hard to imagine,' Henry added.

'Yes.'

They sat in the sitting-room – there were roses on the walls. Thelma had called it 'the lounge'. (You had a lounge in a public place, in a hotel – not in a home.)

Mrs Gadny sipped at the port Henry had given her. 'It's a cosy home you have, Thelma.'

'Thank you, dear.'

'A palace when you think of my old—'

'Oh no—'

'A palace.'

She had kept herself polite all day. She'd shown no sadness at leaving the Terrace (she'd waved to those of the neighbours who'd been watching, as if she'd been royalty); she'd not lingered in her rooms before going, as people were supposed to do. She'd walked out of the house to the waiting car wearing as big a smile as was manageable.

'Henry will carry your cases up to your room.'

Her room had violets on its walls.

'I shall never be able to thank you both—'

'Don't you try to, dear.'

'Dear' seemed to be Thelma's favourite word.

'Don't you *dare* try to.'

Thelma sat beneath a lamp. Mrs Gadny could see the black roots in Thelma's new blonde hair.

'We want you to feel part of our family, dear. Don't we, Henry?'

'Yes.'

Thelma smiled at her.

'I shall try to pay my way.'

Henry said, 'We'll see.'

She still had her pride. In seventy years she had never sunk so low she had to accept charity. 'We *shan't* see, Henry. I shall pay a weekly sum. For my bed and board.'

'Fill your stepmother's glass, Henry. And let us both have another sherry. Talk about money gets me down. You can discuss that some other time. I want us all to have a happy evening.'

The child obviously didn't enjoy being kissed. She wiped her mouth immediately afterwards.

'I'm your father's stepmother, Edna.'

'I know.'

'Speak so you can be heard,' Thelma said.

'I shall be staying with you, Edna.'

'I know.'

'I can hear you now.'

'I know.'

'She's shy with you,' Thelma said, 'but you'll find young Michael shyer.'

He was in the doorway, his head against the door.

'He has phases,' Henry explained. 'I mean, some times he'll be almost friendly, other times not.'

'Come into the room, Michael. Say "Hullo" to your grand-mother.'

Michael took one large step forward. 'Hullo.'

'Hullo, Michael. Haven't you grown?' Michael looked at the carpet. 'Hasn't he grown, Thelma?'

'Yes.' Thelma smiled at her children. 'Go to the bathroom and wash your hands before we eat.'

Edna pushed her brother before her.

Her few old bits of china made the room look almost homely. The bed had a hard mattress. This pleased her: it *was* what she was accustomed to.

Her window overlooked the back garden.

Once between the sheets, she would try to sleep. She would not allow herself any thoughts of the Terrace. The past, as they said, was the past. She was in her new home now. Altogether, she could have done far worse.

The violets looked prettier with only a lamp on them.

She found she could hear Thelma and Henry talking in their bedroom. She got into bed and turned out the light.

Henry had always been a mystery. He'd been the strangest of boys. Why had he asked her here?

She must accustom herself to life in his house. Perhaps, if she really exerted herself, she would overcome her dislike of Thelma. Was it as strong as dislike? She certainly found her manner irritating. The children, too, they had to be considered. There was plenty to occupy her.

She could make out a good many of the words Thelma was saying to Henry. The walls were thin as paper. Houses these days, however fine they looked, were not built to last.

She tested her smile in the bathroom mirror. Yes, yes. She went down to the kitchen.

'You look happy,' Henry said.

'I am.'

Edna stared at her. Mrs Gadny smiled. 'And how is Edna?'

'All right.'

'Where's your brother?'

'My mother's dressing him.'

'At his age?'

'My brother can't help himself. He's a baby.'

That was real spite in the child's voice.

'He's a nice boy. I like him.'

'Do you?'

'Yes.'

'Do you like me?'

'Yes.'

'Why do you?'

'Because you're a little girl—'

'That's no reason.'

'It is.'

'Do you only like me for *that*?'

'*For* that?'

'For being a little girl?'

'Oh no.'

'What else do you like me for?'

It was difficult finding an answer. Edna stared at her as she thought.

'Stop your questions,' Henry said eventually.

Each morning she dusted and polished. Thelma said she was a great help: the work got done in a trice.

She was settling, wasn't she? They liked each other, didn't they? She wasn't in the least like a mother-in-law, was she? But then, if you thought, she *wasn't* a mother-in-law, was she?

She wondered if it was marriage that made Henry slower. He shuffled about, such a load on his feet. His had never been an energetic nature. He hadn't ever joined in games, she remembered, nor had he run much or gone for walks. He'd been slow to learn, too – he'd spent hours at his books. His father, who'd been blessed with a nimble mind, had often lost patience with him.

He seemed to have no energy, no drive.

He was passing her room like an elephant when she called out to him: 'Come and talk to me.'

He sat next to her on the bed. 'Collapsed on to it' would have been more accurate, she thought. She took his hand. 'I want you to know I'm grateful.'

'That's all right.'

The stomach he had on him! And the flesh on his face – his eyes were small as a pig's!

'Poor Henry,' she surprised herself by saying.

'Why poor?'

He knew she didn't mean 'poor' financially: he was safe in insurance.

'Why poor?'

'You look as if you have the miseries.'

'My expression, I suppose.'

She couldn't call to her mind any occasion when Henry had been miserable: she had never seen him cry or lose his temper or shout. And that expression of his, it rarely changed. When he smiled, it was more a smirk his lips made. Had he ever in his life laughed aloud?

'You should know my expression by now.'

'I do, dear.'

'Well, then.' To make matters clear, he added, 'It would take a great deal to upset me.'

His father's death definitely hadn't. Nor, as far as she knew, had his mother's. She wouldn't swear to it: some people kept their feelings hidden. Though she had her doubts that Henry was one of those people.

His hand slid free. He coughed.

'Henry, dear,' she said, 'you're very fortunate.'

'Having Thelma and the children?'

'Yes. And this lovely house.'

'Yes. Yes, I am.'

He scratched at his leg.

'I must go soon, I suppose.'

'I asked you to talk to me.'

'Yes.'

She thought quickly: what can I say to him? She stared at the violets. 'Whose idea was it – the flowers in the rooms?'

'Thelma's.'

The decorative things in the house all stemmed from Thelma. She should know he had no eye for colour except when it came to photographs. He'd put up shelves; he'd helped the men lay the carpets; fitted light sockets: nothing more. He hoped he was a useful kind of person.

'You are.'

'I try to be.'

He'd always breathed loudly.

'And how's your photography going?'

'All right.'

Apart from his work, he had two interests: photography and crime. He seldom talked about them.

'And what about the other?'

'What other?'

'What I call your "morbid" interest.'

'All right.'

On his death-bed he would say he was all right.

'I still have that book.'

When he was sixteen he bought himself a huge brown scrapbook. Instead of filling it with family snaps as any ordinary boy would have done, he cut out pictures of murderers and accounts of their trials and stuck them in.

'The scrapbook?'

'Yes.'

'Do you still stick pictures and things in it?'

'Yes.'

He ran a hand down his nose. He asked her if she had any problems.

'Problems, Henry?'

'About living here?'

'No.'

Thelma's cooking – some of her meals really weighed on you. Edna. The smell of the house.

'No,' she repeated. She didn't wish to appear petty.

'No?'

'No.'

'I want you – *we* want you – to feel part of the family.'

'I do feel part.'

He stood up. He patted his stomach – an act which set Thelma scowling when he did it at table.

'I suppose I must go.'

'Yes, Henry,' she said. 'You go.'

He looked down at her. He was breathing loudly and his arms hung loose.

She suddenly imagined him on top of Thelma, misbehaving himself. How could *she*, scarcely more than a bean-pole, suffer all that weight?

The awful thought went.

Henry said 'Good night'.

He turned, moved towards the door.

She wanted to ask him if he loved Thelma; she wanted to know if he was capable.

The afternoons had to be lived through.

On fine days there was no cause for worry: she walked in the local park, sat by the pond until she felt the cold, made her way slowly home. But she began to dread the rain or those days when the cold was wintry and bitter: it meant the lounge (as Thelma *would* insist on calling the sitting-room) and making conversation.

She sat facing Thelma, longing to be spirited away.

The shopping and cleaning were done; they had taken a light meal – now there were three whole hours to go before the children returned from school.

She would feign a headache later, disappear to her room.

Thelma put down her hospital romance. 'I can only read for

ten-minute stretches. Then the words get jumbled together.'
She took a chocolate from a box on the table by her chair. 'Do
you have that trouble, dear?'

'No. I can read when the mood comes on me. Celia read
aloud to me, the last few years.'

'That must have been nice.'

'It was.'

'Yes, dear.'

That was the most irritating habit, that constant 'dear' of
Thelma's. It came off her tongue like any other word. She might
just as well call her 'sweetheart' or 'darling' or, she laughed,
'precious'.

'I believe you're laughing at me, dear.'

'No, Thelma, not at you. I was thinking of someone I once
worked for. The Honourable Walter Crabbe – not spelt like the
sea-food, he had a "b" and an "e" on the end—'

'What about him?'

'You won't think it funny – in fact, you'll think me daft.
It was just that he always called his wife "precious". Even at
dinner. There I'd be, standing ready to serve, and he'd call down
the table "Cicely, my precious, potatoes?" "A little cabbage,
my precious?" he'd say.'

'It *is* quaint, I'll grant you.'

'He was a kind, thoughtful man for all his airs.'

'I'm sure he was, dear.'

'A gentleman.'

Thelma took another chocolate. She bit into its hard
centre.

Yes, she had no complaints to make about the Honourable Walter. Or the Honourable Cicely. They were thoroughly decent, both of them.

'Were they, dear?'

'Thoroughly.'

She went to them first as a scullery-maid. She was fourteen, fresh from a Hampshire village.

'I still have a bit of country in my voice.'

'I can't say it's struck me. But then, I'm a town girl.'

'You can never really *lose* an accent.'

'Can't you, dear?'

'No.'

Thelma wouldn't believe her, but her wages were nine shillings a month. Imagine! And the work she did – scrubbing, polishing, sewing, learning to cook and to wait at table. She had one free Sunday in four, she recalled, and every other Thursday afternoon off.

Thelma sighed, shook her head.

The letters she wrote home – page upon page upon page. Writing down the things that happened to her seemed as natural as – well, breathing or sleeping. The sad part was, her father and her brother Jim couldn't read or write. She made a vow once that she would try to teach them but nothing came of it. Her mother read the letters to them.

Thelma said something about the rain. Then she put a chocolate in her mouth.

She would talk, whether Madam of the house wanted to hear her or not. What else could she do? Watch her eat? Look out at the rain? Stare at the roses? She would continue until it was time to announce a headache.

She wasn't a scullery-maid long. Mrs Crabbe recognized her worth. Her position improved.

'Did it, dear?'

'Yes. I was allowed to serve vegetables.'

'Were you?'

'Yes.'

Cabinet ministers, famous actors and actresses, dukes, duchesses, lords, ladies, the highest in the land: the finest people there were sat down to eat with the Honourable Mr and Mrs Crabbe.

'Did they? Did they, dear?'

'I stood close to them, Thelma. As close as I am to you.'

'Oh?'

She stayed with them twenty-five years. She remembered having fears of dying an old maid. But she had found Tom, or Tom had found *her*—

'You probably found each other,' Thelma suggested.

'Yes.'

He courted her in a check suit that had a cap to match.

When she finished talking it was past two o'clock. An hour had been killed.

Thelma said she would try another chapter before the children were here to bother her again.

Mrs Gadny looked at her. How much had she heard? Her mind, such as there was, must have wandered.

'I have a pain in my head, Thelma. I shall go to my room and lie down.'

*

She'd had a nightmare. White hands in the dark.

Had she screamed?

She listened. Silence through the house.

Whose hands were they? Were they someone's? She hadn't been able to tell if they were Celia's, Tom's: she hadn't thought to look hard.

But you didn't think to look hard when you dreamed. Dreaming simply happened.

No arms or elbows. No other parts.

'I dread to think what he'll be like in a few years,' Thelma said. 'His head's never out of a book now. When he can read properly he'll be as bad as his father for talking to. I can see we shall be calling him "The Professor".'

The boy had been crying, for no reason it seemed. The picture-book had quietened him.

'Have you noticed with Henry – if he has a paper or one of his books on criminals?'

'Yes.'

'Always when I want to talk to him, ask his advice. He could be in China.'

'Yes.'

'Young Michael will be as bad. Edna's the sensible child. He's the moody one.'

Edna took one of her mother's chocolates.

'Would you like a present, Michael?'

He was smiling at some picture.

'Answer your grandmother, young Michael.'

'Would you like a present?'

'Yes.'

'Yes, what?'

'Please.'

'Come with me.' She offered her hand.

'Go with your grandmother.'

He ignored her hand. He followed her upstairs.

'Would you like some books for when you're older?'

'Yes. Please.'

They were in her room.

'Sit on the bed, Michael.'

He pulled up his socks before he did so.

'My daughter read lots of books. Hundreds. I've kept some of them. They'll only rot. I shan't read them any more.'

She was used to being read to; she had taken in more of the stories when Celia read them to her.

The books were in a pile in the wardrobe. She managed to lift them out and carry them to the bedside table.

'*Jane Eyre*. That one's a kind of love story.' She laughed. 'Boys don't take to love stories until they're much older. Some never take to them.'

Michael stared at the inscription. '"Her book",' he said.

'It says "Celia Gadny. Her book." That's what's written.'

'"Celia Gadny. Her book."'

'Quite right. Your aunt. You met her twice.'

'"Celia Gadny. Her book",' he said again.

'*The Pilgrim's Progress*. Look, Michael. This one has pictures.'

'"Celia Gadny. Her book."'

It was something for him to say.

'Yes, Michael.' She'd often chuckled at the picture Michael was looking at: whoever had done it must have copied it from a photo – Christian looked like Ramon Navarro without his moustache.

'*Treasure Island*. Long John Silver, Michael? You know him?'

'No.'

'He's a terror. One leg. A parrot on his shoulder. A pirate to the life.'

She gave him those books of Celia's she had kept. Some of them were of poetry – the boy might take to it. She hadn't, all life long. Celia had tried poems on her – simple ones, she'd said, about birds and trees. They'd passed straight through her head. A verse on a card was a different case: it was intended for one person from another, it carried a loving message.

She hesitated before giving him the last book in the pile.

'This one, Michael. This one is beautiful.'

The boy was called 'Pip'. He helped a convict escape. He met a girl and a very odd woman who lived in a big house. The odd woman went about the place in her wedding-dress because she'd been left in the lurch on the great day, which was before the story started.

And then what?

Pip becomes rich in the city and the convict he helped when he was small turns up one night. Yes. And later still there comes the scene she and Celia had once cried over: the convict gets captured and Pip realizes how much he owes to him. Yes. He had a name, too – he wasn't known as a convict. Think without looking. 'Magpie', was it? Something similar.

'This is a beautiful book.'

She didn't seem capable of getting the boy to look at her. 'Put your head up.'

'"Celia Gadny. Her book."'

'Never mind that. You'll enjoy this story one day, Michael, when you're old enough to appreciate it.'

He counted the letters in the title. He stopped at ten.

'Eleven,' she said.

'Eleven.'

'Twelve.'

'Twelve.'

'Thirteen comes after.'

But his mind was off. '"Her book",' he said. '"Her book".'

'Yes, Michael.'

He might grow into the kind of man who would despise a woman like Thelma.

He arranged the books around him on the bed.

'What's she given you?' Edna had to be wherever her brother was.

'I've given him some books.'

'What books?'

'They belonged to my daughter.'

'I don't care.'

'As Michael seems to go for reading—' She stopped. The girl was looking at her with disgust.

'What is it, Edna? Is my slip showing? Staring at people is rude. Hasn't your mother told you?'

'You have grey skin,' Edna said.

She supposed it was damp that caused the wallpaper to bulge in places. They should have had more sense than to paper a bathroom.

She lay in the bath. She sponged her legs gently.

Number Ninety-six was the only house in the Terrace to have a bathroom. Mrs Barber and her Rose made use of it twice a week.

She closed her eyes and saw the tramp-woman.

… A black coat that was turning green, bandaged legs, bags containing old clothes and food scraps…

She put out a hand for the soap, took it from the rack.

… One tooth in the middle of her mouth…

She rubbed the soap against the sponge.

… The bandages rotting, rusty safety-pins keeping them in place. Toes jutting out of shoes…

She returned the soap to the rack, put the sponge to her face.

… Pigeons perching on her shoulders, perching on her hands, on her head…

—Scum of the earth, Mrs Barber said. Move away from our terrace.

The tramp-woman lit her clay pipe.

—You lower the tone of the district. Doesn't she, Faith?

'Yes. You're not fit to—'

She opened her eyes. She sat up in the bath and listened. The children might have heard her talking.

Edna Gadny should have seen the tramp-woman. Her skin really *was* grey.

They were off to spend Sunday with Mr and Mrs Nutley, Thelma's parents. Mrs Gadny sat between the children in the back of the car.

'We chose the right day,' Thelma said. The weather was spring-like, trees beginning to bud.

'It's a change for you, dear. You must get very bored at Roselea with only me for company in the day time.'

'I don't get bored, Thelma. Not the slightest bit. No.'

'It's a change, anyway. You haven't seen my Mum since our wedding, have you?'

No, she hadn't seen Thelma's mother since the wedding. She wished she could remind Thelma that the question had been answered on three separate occasions since Mrs Nutley's telephone call of a week ago.

'She's our proper Gran,' Edna said.

Thelma said hastily, 'Edna means that Henry's only your stepson, while I'm Mum's rightful daughter—'

'I know, Thelma. I know what you mean, Edna.' She patted the child's knee.

'Remember, young Michael, I want you to speak to your

grandparents today. I don't want you sulking in corners. You just be sociable, like your sister.'

'He's a shy boy. Some boys *are*. Henry's father – my Tom – was shy of people all his life, wasn't he, Henry?'

'I suppose he was.'

'You suppose! You know quite well. He hated company. He hardly spoke to the people he worked with for so many years. He sat in his chair most evenings and Celia and me, we'd forget he was there. His head was in his Bible – or he'd be staring into the fire—'

'Yes, dear.'

'Your Michael probably has the same sort of nature. He'll be a thoughtful one.'

'So long as he's sensible as well.'

'He will be.'

'We don't know, do we, dear? We can only guess. Everything rests with fate.'

Fate might bring him, like her Celia, to an early grave. 'Lift your head up, Michael,' she said softly.

'Yes, young Michael, do as you're told. Allow your grand-parents to see your face for once.'

'Edna's wearing Georgie's ribbon, isn't she?' Georgie, Mrs Nutley's dog, had pink ribbon tied in a bow between his ears. 'He's a boisterous little chap is Georgie. He's a chihuahua, Faith.'

The dog attempted to bite Michael's ankle. The boy, back-ing away, began to cry.

'He hates the male sex, does Georgie. He won't even tolerate Mr Nutley – will he, Maurice?'

'No.'

'He barks his little head off if I try to go anywhere without him.' She added, in a whisper, nudging Mrs Gadny, 'I even have to take him to the toilet with me. I can't leave him with Mr Nutley for a moment – he'd plague his life.'

Michael screamed.

'Oh, Michael, what a thing to do! Are you frightened of my little dog?'

Michael nodded, sniffed.

'You don't want your son becoming a cissy, do you, Henry?' She called to the dog: 'Come to Mummy, Georgie. Leave the cry-baby alone.'

Mrs Nutley bent down, took Georgie into her arms.

'Shall we all go into the house? Do you notice the name, Faith?'

A wooden sign hung from the porch.

'As you see, it says "The Haven". That's how we think of our home – a haven, a haven of rest. Mr Nutley and myself put our life savings into buying it. We wanted somewhere snug for our last years.'

'Maurice,' Mrs Nutley said when the greetings were done and coats hung in the hall, 'take your grandson to see the animals.' Mr Nutley was nothing more than a boy in his heart – the old idiot kept white mice and rabbits in his shed at the bottom of the back lawn. He spent hours with the blessed creatures – she had often considered divorcing him, citing them as co-respondents. 'The shed is forbidden territory, isn't it, Georgie?' She gave the dog a finger to play with. 'Don't lick Mummy's varnish off, naughty one.'

'When are we eating?'

'Your stomach, Maurice – it's never long out of your mind. We'll eat at twelve. Now then, let's have some organization. Don't stand about, Maurice, take your grandson off before Georgie sends him into a fit. I shall show Henry's stepmother over the house. Would Faith like that?'

'Yes.'

'Good. You, Thelma, take Edna and that husband of yours into the lounge.'

'Impressed?'

'Yes.'

'We found most of our ideas in American magazines. The kitchen came straight from a picture in *Luxury Homes*.'

'Oh?'

Luxury Homes? Luxury Factories.

'The picture decided us. It had to be ours, cost regardless.'

Red lights, green lights, switches, dials.

'Well, Faith, this is our last port of call. Our guest room. Your inspection's completed.'

'Thank you for showing me, Mrs—'

She'd forgotten Thelma's maiden name. The embarrassment.

'For God's sake, Faith, you know I'm Marjorie. You don't have to be all stiff and formal with me.'

'No.'

Black-outs hit everyone at times.

'We're not exactly old friends, I grant you, but we are part of a family. In a sort of way… Where were we? Yes. The guest room. Whenever you feel like making use of it, just give a tinkle or drop me a card and I'll have it made ready for you. A stay here would be a nice change. I'm sure there are occasions when that husband of Thelma's makes you wish you were anywhere but Roselea. Or that boy's snivelling – I'm sure the noise must work on your nerves. It does mine… You *will* stay soon, won't you?'

'Thank you. Yes. Thank you.'

'Meanwhile—'

Yes. Nutley. Yes.

'Are you with me, Faith?'

'Yes.'

'Well, dear… Listen. Before we go down, I want us to have a talk. Woman to woman.'

'Talk? What about?'

'You.'

The sun was on Mrs Nutley's glasses. Mrs Gadny couldn't see her eyes.

'You look so surprised. A talk, Faith, only a talk. From what I've heard, you need a sorting-out.'

'A—?'

'Sorting-out. Sit somewhere. All the chairs are comfortable.'

She chose the couch. Mrs Nutley arranged herself on a ledge by the window.

'Stay in Mummy's lap, Georgie.'

Mrs Nutley looked down at her. 'How old am I, Faith?'

'Old?'

'Guess.'

'Sixty.'

'Sixty-two.'

'Oh?'

'I put it to you – do I look as old as that?'

She could say 'Yes.'

'No.'

'No flattery?'

'No.'

'And how old are you? Seventy?'

'Seventy-one – come September.'

'September's months ahead. You're seventy then, Faith – and frankly, my dear – and you are not to take offence because I say it in your interest – you look it.'

'Do I?'

'Yes. And I shall tell you why.'

'It's no crime.' She became aware that she was nodding. She willed her head to remain still before she said 'It's no crime, looking one's age.'

'I didn't say it was.'

Mrs Nutley's eyes were on her – she could see them now. They were pricing every piece of clothing she wore. 'What's this – this sorting-out?'

'I hesitate to tell you, I truly do. I'm the first to appreciate the suffering you've had. And I know, dear, the extent of it – losing those you cherish most in the world. Thelma and me, both being women, see more clearly than your stepson could – or Mr Nutley could, to be honest – just what you've gone through. Men never understand the deep feelings we women—'

'My Tom was a very—'

'As a general rule. Your husband was the exception. I'm glad you mentioned him.'

'Why glad?'

'You think why, dear.'

She could scream so the ceiling cracked: Why should *I* think why? She asked, quietly: 'Why glad?'

'Think, Faith.'

'I can't.'

'You mentioned your husband, Faith. He's been dead some years – am I right?'

'Yes.'

'I'm sure he was a fine man—'

'He was.'

'And your daughter, I remember from Thelma's wedding, seemed a sweet girl—'

'She was.'

'Allow me to be blunt. You mentioned your husband because you're living in the past. You're living with the dead. And that is why – and I say it for your good – you look every minute of your seventy years.'

She had waited on cabinet ministers, dukes and duchesses,

the highest in the land. She had been respected by people of the calibre of the Honourable Mr and Mrs Crabbe.

'Have I been rude?'

She'd been loved by a good husband.

'Have you taken exception?'

'No.'

'You're wise not to.'

And here she was, listening to Mrs Nutley, a woman with blue hair.

'May I go on?'

In a strange house. Switches and dials.

'May I?'

'Yes.'

'I say this in all humility. I say this in your interest. You *must* get out of yourself.'

In a luxury home.

'You must. Life's for living.'

Mrs Nutley stroked the dog, asleep in her lap. 'Georgie's having a snooze, crafty fellow.'

'Is he?'

'He's tired himself.' Mrs Nutley smiled at her. 'To return to the advice I'm giving you. Do you know what I do when feeling low? Do you know what I think of?'

'No.'

'Cripples.'

'Cripples?'

'Yes. Those who can't walk without the aid of irons, sticks. I read a piece on them in one of my magazines. It was by that beautiful man who writes so movingly about our royal family. He said the sight of those poor, maimed people lifted his heart.'

'Oh?'

'He said we must all think of the brave smiles they wear in the face of adversity.'

'Oh?'

'"Oh", yes! You try it, Faith. Whenever a mood of sorrow comes over you, seizes you, just stop for a moment and consider the cripples. Or the blind, or deaf. Then you'll see how fortunate you are.'

'Will I?'

'Yes, dear.'

'Mrs Nutley, Mrs Nutley, I don't think I *am* unhappy. I try not to live in the past. I busy myself about Thelma's house, keep my mind free of worries. Why you should give me advice, I can't imagine.'

'Because my daughter asked me to.'

'She asked you?'

'Yes. She could hardly do it herself, could she? A young woman advising an – a mature one? She realized, sensible girl, that tact was called for.'

'What did she say to you?'

'She's worried, Faith, on your behalf.'

'Why?'

'She says you seldom smile. She says you look depressed, particularly in the afternoons.'

From one o'clock to four o'clock. The roses on the walls.

'Oh no.'

'She says you sit there for long stretches, staring. And when you talk, she says, it's never about the present day. You act like a ghost, in her view.'

'Do I?'

'Yes. Come alive, Faith. You could look years younger.'

'I don't want to.'

'Yes, you do. Was there ever a woman in this world who wanted to look her age? I don't believe so.'

If Mr Nutley died, would Mrs Nutley think of cripples? Or would she wander from room to room in her luxury home? Would she remove her butterfly-winged glasses so that she could cry more freely?

Mrs Gadny smiled.

'Faith, you're smiling!'

'Yes.'

Would her dog stop barking? Would the animals starve in their shed?

Mrs Gadny wanted to laugh.

'Faith, you're laughing!'

'Yes.'

'You've come to your senses?'

'Yes.'

'Seen the truth in my words?'

'Yes.'

'Good. Good girl.'

*

Wasn't her Mum a miracle?

Yes.

So young at sixty-five.

Sixty-five?

Not a year under.

Oh?

The figure of a model. So trim.

Yes. Yes.

'Did you notice, dear, how little she ate?'

'Yes.'

'Don't deafen me, dear. While we were all gorging.' Were we?

One day she would turn on Thelma, when their politeness had worn off, when she felt less of a guest in her house—

'I feel refreshed for seeing her.'

—turn on her and let her know that in seventy years she had never tasted a fouler meal. Beef should be roasted lightly. Roast beef, Thelma, is the better for having blood in it.

'She was very cross with me, Henry, for not complimenting her on her new specs…'

'Was she, dear?' her husband asks.

'Yes, she was.'

Your mother, Thelma, with all her gadgets, her switches, her dials, is an even worse cook than you.

'Should my sight ever fail, I should choose a pair like hers.'

'Oh Thelma—'

'Dear?'

'Oh Thelma, look what Michael's done. He's fallen asleep in the crook of my arm. I've only this minute seen him.'

'Well. Well. You *are* honoured.'

'Granny Nutley's pretty,' Edna sang quietly. 'Granny Nutley's pretty.'

'You *are* honoured,' Henry said.

'I don't know about honoured, the way he's behaved today. Sulk, sulk, sulk. I wish he could be like other boys, Henry. I wish he could be more normal.'

'He looks content now, Thelma.'

'Does he, dear?'

'A cherub.'

The radiator's gurgle woke her.

She pushed the sheets away and left the bed. She removed her nightdress. It was the blue one Celia had given her two Christmasses back.

She looked down at her breasts. Dolores, Tom once told her, had them the size of oranges.

Her belly stuck out.

The tops of her legs were dark with veins. Purple ones, running in and out of each other.

'Am I old?' she whispered.

—Yes, you are, Mrs Nutley said. What a belly, what veins.

'Let me see yours. Your breasts, your—'

She was standing like Charlie Chaplin – left foot going left, right going right.

She heard Thelma wake Henry. She heard her telling him to listen.

She walked to the wall. She smiled as she put her ear against a violet.

Henry cleared his throat.

Mrs Nutley had seen her dressed. Of course. No woman in this world would see her naked.

People said she dressed well. Sensibly, as became her age. Mrs Barber, Mrs Rennett, Mrs Fields, Mrs Dumsday – they all said.

'Henry,' she heard Thelma say after some considerable time, 'I won't have you doing things to me while she's living in the next room. Any noise can be heard. You should have thought of that before you invited her here.'

She got into her dressing-gown. She went to the window, opened it. She filled her lungs with God's good air.

'Why did you marry Thelma?'

'Why?'

'Yes, Henry.'

'Why does anyone marry?'

'Was love the reason?'

'You're asking me some strange questions.'

'Do you love her, Henry?'

'Love? Such a moon-struck sort of word that is.'

'No. No, Henry.'

'Here's Christie. I've given him six pages.'

'That face. Whatever went on in his head?'

'His secret.'

'Yes.'

'Thelma hates this book, even though she's never looked at it. She's often threatened to burn it. I lock it in my darkroom during the day.'

'You don't trust her?'

'Not with this. If she got at this in one of her rages, tore it to bits, years of work would be wasted. I daren't take the risk.'

'You think she would? Tear it? Burn it?'

'If she wanted to hurt me, she would. If she wanted to make me mad.'

'You're similar to me, Thelma, in one respect.'

'What's that, dear?'

'In not having many friends.'

'Friends, dear? I have plenty.'

'Why don't they visit you? Or you them?'

'They live in the country. Or some distance away. The Marshalls, the Platt twins.'

'Oh?'

'And abroad. I have a friend from school who's in America. In Texas.'

'I see.'

'So I'm not similar to you. I receive a lot of correspondence, dear. I can show you if you don't believe me.'

'Naturally I believe you. Naturally I do.'

'Good.'

'I had several acquaintances, Thelma. Mrs Rennett, Mrs Fields, Mrs Dumsday. But Mrs Barber was my one true friend.'

'Was she?'

'Yes. And Ada, the cook for the Crabbes.'

'That sounds funny – the cook for the Crabbes.'

'Does it? Ada died before the war.'

'The phrase, dear. I don't mean *she* was funny.'

'Oh? I see, Thelma.'

'Good.'

'You could say that Mr and Mrs Crabbe were friends.'

'Could you?'

'Thinking about it, though, they were always a trifle distant with those out of their class. They were thoughtful, they studied me, they were kind to me but – but—'

'At a distance?'

'Yes. At a distance.'

'I would have spat on them.'

'What?'

'I would have spat on them.'

'Thelma!'

'I hate being condescended to.'

'What?'

'Don't keep saying "What?", dear.'

'They didn't condescend, Thelma. They never ever did. You must understand: I was only a maid, a servant – they were titled people.'

'Yes, dear. Yes, dear.'

*

'What do you call the doll?'

'Jane.'

'Jane?'

'She's the plain one. Can't you see?'

'Yes.'

'If she was a person no one would marry her.'

'How unkind of you, Edna.'

'It's the truth. Diana and Ruby are the beautiful dolls. They're the ones to look at.'

'They'll marry?'

'If they were real, they would.'

'Diana and Ruby.'

'I told you their names when you came here to live but you couldn't have been listening.'

'I was. I was.'

'You don't listen much. I've watched you.'

'I listen to everything—'

'No, you don't.'

'Yes, I do, Edna.'

'No, you don't. Otherwise my mother wouldn't put on her loud voice when she speaks to you. Like she does to my father. She never speaks loud to me.'

'It's time for your bath.'

'Michael goes first. You can bath him if you want to. I'm old enough to do it myself.'

*

The tramp-woman walked up the gravel path. She stopped in front of the house. She said 'The Haven, The Haven, The Haven' and smiled broadly, her one tooth showing. She pressed a button by the door and then the chimes sounded – a recognizable tune, an old one.

Mrs Nutley appeared, dressed in blue. 'To match your lovely hair,' said the tramp-woman, smiling again.

'How nice of you to say. Do come in.'

The door had vanished, and the hall. Mrs Nutley stood next to the tramp-woman in the middle of the lounge. 'There's luxury carpet beneath your feet, my dear.' 'Is there?' 'My goodness, your shoes have holes!' 'Always did, Ma'am, always did.' 'There's luxury carpet beneath your feet.'

The tramp-woman handed Mrs Nutley two large bags. She lit her clay pipe. Mrs Nutley coughed. 'If you wish to smoke, go into the garden.'

The tramp-woman undid the remaining button on her black coat. She lifted her dress and showed Mrs Nutley her knees. Then she squatted.

The tramp-woman made water on the luxury carpet. The pool spread. Mrs Nutley said, 'A flood! You're causing a flood!'

The tramp-woman laughed.

Waking, she looked into Henry's face.

'You woke us with your laughter.'

'Laughter, Henry?'

'Yes.'

'Yes, dear,' Thelma shouted from her bedroom.

'I was laughing?'

'Loudly. Fit to burst.'

'The tramp-woman. The dream.'

'I guessed you were dreaming—'

'You remember, Henry? The tramp-woman?'

'Who?'

'Oh, you must. She sat on the wall outside the paint shop on the corner of the Terrace. A dirty thing, she was.'

'I remember.'

'Yes. Celia spoke to her once – against my wishes – and found out she was Irish. As if she could have come from any other country! I swear no race on earth is as dirt-ridden.'

'We called her "Granny Grunt".'

'You did, too.'

'What was she up to in the dream?'

'Up to?'

'To make you laugh?'

'She—'

'She?'

She peed on Thelma's mother's carpet.

'She—'

'Tell me. Perhaps I'll enjoy it.'

Pigs might fly.

'Why the delay?'

'My nightdress is soaking.'

'Sweat, I imagine.'

'It can't be.'

'The weather's warmer.'

'Oh God. Oh no. Oh God, Henry.'

'What is it?'

'Lift the bed-clothes. Let me see.'

The sheets had yellow patches.

'Oh God.'

Her hands rushed to her face.

'Look, Henry. What I've done.'

Henry stared. She saw him through the gaps between her fingers.

'Henry. Henry.' She thought she sounded like someone speaking into a funnel.

'Dear me. Dear me,' Henry said.

She lowered her hands. The sheets were yellow. And Henry's face. And the violets.

'I've wet the bed.'

'I'm afraid you have.'

'Through to the mattress.'

'Never mind.'

The nightdress stuck to her legs.

'You'd better move,' Henry said.

'Yes.'

'I'll help you.'

She stood beside the bed. She shivered.

'I must wash myself.'

'Yes.'

'I must put on something dry.'

'Go along. I'll cope.'

'Don't tell Thelma' came out of her mouth before she could stop it.

'All right.'

'I'm sorry, Henry.'

'All right.'

She wanted to thank him for not looking disgusted. 'Henry,' she said, 'do you know when I last did that?'

'When?'

'Sixty years ago, I should think. Years back, anyway, when I was a girl in the country. My father shook pepper on to the sheets and rubbed my nose in it. It cured me.'

'Did it?'

'Until now.'

'Don't worry.'

She saw herself in the wardrobe mirror. 'What a thing to do,' she said to her reflection. 'At your age.'

Thelma stood in the doorway. 'What have you asked Henry not to tell me?'

'I want to tell you myself, Thelma—'

'Your nightdress!'

'I've had an accident.'

Thelma joined Henry by the bed.

'You don't have to tell me. I can see quite clearly what you've done.'

'An accident—'

'The bathroom is only at the end of the passage.'

'I know it is. Of course I know.'

'Too tired to move, were you?'

'No.'

'You just lay there, instead of stirring yourself—'

'No, Thelma.'

'She was dreaming,' Henry said.

'Dreaming? Of the sea or something?'

'Yes. I was on a boat, Thelma; it started to sink—'

'You can spare me the story.'

'I was explaining—'

'The sheets are probably ruined.'

'I'll wash them, Thelma. I'll scrub them clean.'

'They smell awful. They stink.'

'I'll wash them, Thelma. They can hang out in the sun.'

'Help me, Henry, to strip the bed.'

'And I'll scrub the mattress.'

'Ruined. Look at it. Ruined.'

'I'll buy you a new one, Thelma. I'll pay for the damage.'

'You make me angry, standing there in that wet dress. Go to the bathroom. Get yourself looking decent again.'

She bought four bunches of anemones from the flowerseller at the gate. Two for Celia, two for Tom. Reds and purples and mauves and pinks.

She wore her Sunday suit. Her hair was freshly permed, curls all in place.

She took the pots from the graves, filled them with water from the tap. When the flowers were arranged to her satisfaction, she stood back to admire them.

Two white stones. Two pots of flowers. Two plots of grass. Celia Gadny. Thomas Gadny.

Rest In Peace. Rest In Peace.

Dead. Dead.

'Both of you.'

Tom and Celia were under the earth, dirt above and around and below them. Tom would be nothing but bone now and Celia – the thought came swiftly – would have turned black.

—Rotting, Mother.

Tom clasped his stomach. He had on his brown suit with the thin stripe, brown shoes, socks the colour of French mustard.

—My guts, he said. Pain's tearing at my guts.

And the ambulance came and carried him off.

'Tom, love.'

She hugged herself to keep out the cold. Her handbag dropped open.

The ambulance bell brought the neighbours to their doors. They watched Tom leave the house on a stretcher. She noticed Mrs Rennett, a strong Catholic, cross herself.

—A show, Tom said. Brightens their lives.

'Don't waste your breath.'

He smiled.

Voices came to her, a babble.

The uniformed man shut the doors of the ambulance. The noise ended.

She closed her eyes, blotting out the past and the two graves. She pinched her arm to test that she was still alive. The gloomy thoughts must moulder.

She opened her eyes. She heard Celia cough.

—The white cells eat the red ones. Doctor Bicknall made

her a pot of tea: that was the kind of man he was – thoughtful, considerate. And he handed her a plate of digestive biscuits. The tea-set was antique – she *knew*, the Crabbes hadn't exactly bought their china in Woolworth's.

A blue castle, blue trees, a blue man and woman on a boat in a lake. Definitely antique.

Celia coughed, louder, her whole body shaking.

—My wife's made a sponge. Would you like some sponge? Thank you. Yes. It's feather-light.

—Take a piece home.

Thank you.

'Thank you, Doctor.'

—I offer you no comfort, Mrs Gadny. There's none I can give. The disease is incurable. Celia will die.

22 Painter Street.

—No comfort.

A hiss from the gas fire.

—At least with cancer there's *some* hope. Traced early enough. He wrapped the slice of sponge in grease-proof paper.

The wind made her skirt rise. She heard a laugh. Turning her head, she saw a tiny man trimming the grass by the path.

'I can see you!'

She pushed her skirt down, held it firmly against her. She'd been told by someone that dwarfs had dirty minds, on account of their height being on a level. It was Mrs Barber – she'd told her. That dwarf from the council estate, him with the big blotch across his face, had once made a suggestion to Rose on the top of a bus.

—I shan't bring a case, Faith, not with him the way he is. I couldn't find it in me to be so cruel. Anyway, Rose told me she called him a filthy little sod. That will give his brain something to chew over.

Yes.

—I told Rose off for using bad language in public. 'Sod' means 'earth', she said right back. What's bad about it?

Rose Barber should have died.

'You'll lose your valuables!'

'I beg your pardon?'

'Your bag's hanging open.'

Yes, it was. 'Thank you.'

'If you've money to spare, it can blow in my direction.'

'I've none to spare, I'm sorry to say.'

'You haven't been here for six weeks, have you?'

'No.'

'I thought I hadn't seen you. I've given your graves a nice trim.'

'Thank you. I'm grateful.'

'I'll watch them for you.'

She offered the dwarf a half-crown.

'You keep it, dear. I'm only doing my job. The borough pays me for my services.'

'Don't stand on pride.'

'No, dear. Two-and-six is two-and-six. You keep it.'

'Goodbye,' she said, and walked away.

She rested a moment by the gate. The path was steep. She was breathless.

'I *am* old,' she said.

The dwarf's cheeks and nose were blotched. The dwarf who tended the graves.

She had spoken to him, looked at him, and she hadn't seen.

'For the life of me,' Thelma said to Henry, 'I don't understand the state she's in. Now you'll ask me what state do I mean, won't you, because it hasn't struck you?'

'She *has* been on edge—'

'On edge? I'll say on edge. Think of me, Henry, trapped in this house all day, stuck here with *her*.'

'What's wrong?'

'Will you listen if I tell you? Will you take it in?'

'It *is* late. Shouldn't we sleep?'

'The weight on my mind, I doubt if I could have a proper night's rest.'

'Don't be so dramatic.'

'Honestly, things never seem to affect you. If there was an earthquake at the end of the street, you'd just stand and gape—'

'It isn't likely to happen.'

'If it did.'

A rustle of sheets.

'Thelma—'

Silence.

'Thelma, what's wrong?'

'Will you listen?'

'Yes.'

'Not interrupt?'

'No.'

Silence.

'The truth is I can't bear the strain. It's becoming too much for me. One day soon I'll crack and do something I shall regret. I'll lose patience, I'll scream at her, I might even hit her. I can't put it into words, I haven't the gift, but I see her sitting opposite me sometimes, wrapped up in her past, and I frighten myself at the thought that I want to knock her into sense – lash out at her.'

'Lash out?'

'Yes. I feel I want to really go for her.' Thelma laughed. 'Only sometimes, Henry. Usually when I have one of my heads. Oh, she annoys me. She drums her fingers on the arm of that chair – thump, thump, thump. I get so keyed up with my nerves I practically count the minutes till Edna and young Michael come home.'

'You should have said before—'

'I've been trying, Henry, to grow to like her. Mainly for your sake. It was you who felt sorry for her – not that I didn't, but I wasn't what you could call in love with the idea of asking her to live with us, as you may or may not remember.'

There was another silence before Henry said he remembered.

'My intuition told me the two of us wouldn't hit it off. I'm still young, Henry. I don't want to be reminded most of the day of – of what might happen to me. Compare her to my mother – look how she wears her years. She refuses, absolutely refuses, to grow old. She doesn't mope—'

'She hasn't lost her husband and her daughter, Thelma.'

'If she did lose Father and me, she'd still cope with life. She'd manage.'

'Perhaps.'

'No "perhaps" – she would.'

'All right.'

'She is good in some ways – your stepmother – I admit. She helps me do the housework; she's looked after the children the few times we've gone out; she pays her way – I admit all that. Though I'm not completely happy about leaving her with the children—'

'Why not?'

'The effect on them. It's bad for them having a woman as miserable as she is—'

'Miserable?'

'You're worse than her for questions tonight. Yes, Henry, miserable. You don't see her during the day – you're away from it. Because it's in the afternoons that her moods reach their peak. Edna comes home from school all happy and bright and what does she see? She sees her staring into space… And the mention of Edna leads me to another point. Your stepmother makes it quite plain that she doesn't approve of my daughter. Oh, yes.'

'You're right.'

'Ah! You've seen?'

'Yes.'

'You're so cagey, Henry, I rarely know what you see or think.'

'But she appears to favour young Michael—'

'What I was about to say. And you know why she favours him?'

'Why?'

'Because he's sullen. He's like her for that: you see how often I have to scold him for not concentrating on what he's doing. How he went off tonight in the middle of the meal, his face all moony. God knows what he can be thinking when he does that. Miss Rivers at the school said he's still behind with his lessons. She said we might have to get a specialist to him some day. I love him, Henry, he's my son, but I only wish he was more like other boys. It can't be a phase, as you always maintain, it's lasted too long, this constant crying and sulkiness.'

'I'll talk with Miss Rivers. I'll talk with the doctor.'

'You must. Now, Henry, while we're on the subject of young Michael, consider – you consider – the effect her moods must have on him.'

'As much as he likes anybody, I almost think he likes her—'

'He likes her for one reason. She spoils him. She gives him many more sweets than she does Edna. And I'll never forgive her for the way she gave him those books. "Would you like a present?" she said to him, as though Edna didn't exist. Not, mind you, it was a present worth having – a pile of old-fashioned stories he won't ever read. Nothing modern, nothing sensible.'

'Celia's books.'

'Who else's?'

—I galloped, Dirck galloped, we galloped all three, Celia recited, her face shining. At the end of the poem the schoolgirls clapped and the headmistress presented her with the book.

—I've seldom heard the good news brought so well, the headmistress told her. The girls and the parents laughed.

Thelma said, 'She never mentions you as a child.'

'Why should she?'

'You're her husband's son. You lived under the same roof.'

'I wasn't close to her. Nor was I close to Dad.'

'Unnatural, Henry. As I once said to you.'

'How it was.'

'You stay so calm.'

Even when Tom took off his belt and beat him. He stayed calm then. Tom went berserk, thrashed the boy's bum until it was raw.

Henry buttoned up his trousers. He walked out to the landing, looked at her. Not the trace of a tear on his face.

—Henry, was it painful?

His smirk for an answer. He walked past her, down the stairs. Tom came out of the bedroom.

—Silly thing to ask the boy, Faith. I gave him eight strokes. You saw the colour of his arse.

He would have said more but he began to cry. He loathed himself after one of his outbursts, was morose for weeks on end. It shamed him, too – his wife seeing him weep.

Henry spoke slowly. 'A lot of people, Thelma, pretend they're close. In families, I mean.'

'Now I'm to have a lecture.'

'I was merely saying. Dad never pretended to me. He didn't show me any dislike but he wasn't affectionate. He was an honest man.'

'He may have been. He wasn't much else. You got where you are without his help—'

'I'm glad I have. I feel the better for it.'

'He should have done his duty by you.'

'I wouldn't let him. I wanted to make my own way. Which is what I've done. In a year I shall be manager of the branch.'

'What?'

'Manager of—'

'When did you hear?'

'Last month.'

'Last month! And you couldn't tell me earlier.'

'I've told you now.'

'You amaze me. You do. Amaze me.'

'The official announcement isn't until July. A dinner is going to be held. We shall go to it together.'

'You wanted to surprise me?'

'Yes. Yes.'

'Well, thank you.'

Madam will be worse now. Chocolates will be ordered by the cartload.

'I shall have a substantial rise.'

'Wonderful.'

In boxes tied with ribbon. Carried to the door by pageboys.

'I want us to live in a house like The Haven. With a kitchen all shiny.'

The switches. The dials.

'Can we, one day?'

'In time.'

'In time, yes. When you're secure as manager. I've come to hate Roselea. I'm bored in it. I want a new house to decorate.'

'You will have. In time. Shall we sleep now?'

'Yes, yes. Go to sleep, Henry. You must have worn yourself out. You've actually talked to me this evening. You've said more than your customary four words.'

'She's been hopping around tonight as if she were crippled.'

—Think of cripples.

'Young Michael kicked her. Naturally, he won't tell me why he did. And she doesn't know.'

'You've asked him?'

'Credit me with some intelligence, Henry.'

'I've been busy with my figures tonight, I—'

'I was a fool, a fool, to let her take him out.'

The white hands woke her. She was being smothered by them. She knew she hadn't screamed. There wasn't enough air in her body. She inhaled deeply – three times, four times – until she was rested.

She turned on the bedside lamp. The clock said five thirty. Celia coughed.

—Mother.

Sheets up to her chin.

'You're dead.'

And so was Tom. She had placed anemones in pots.

She shook with fright. 'They're dead.'

In the cemetery with the dwarf.

She tried to scream but no sound came.

It was real. A certainty, a fact. She felt dazed from thinking of it. Worse than a blow on the head. For weeks – how long? – the thought had been mixed up with other thoughts: getting through the day, talking, eating, dressing, trying to sleep.

And not being able to read, not even a paper. And watching the television – grey dots. And walking in the park.

And seeing the chocolates go into the mouth: jaw up, jaw down.

She stood by the bed. The pain beneath her right knee had gone.

Was she at Number Ninety-six? The fruit bowl was by the window; there were the Coronation mugs; the vase from Mrs Crabbe.

She looked at the photographs on the quilt. The soldiers at Wipers were the colour of weak tea. Tom stared at her.

Celia at the zoo. Which animal was in the cage?

Now she was in the hall. The barometer at Windy.

She sniffed. This house smelled of scent, not polish.

—I'll dispose of your furniture, Henry said. You're being sensible. Make a new start with us.

—At Roselea, Thelma said.

'Ninety-six.'

—At Roselea.

A Jew-boy had bought the houses in the Terrace.

—Thank you, Mrs Gadny, for leaving without a fuss. Some of your neighbours have been very difficult. I can't throw them out, can I? I shall have to wait for them to pass on. And I have such plans for these houses—

She heard the cough, and started to sob.

'My God,' Thelma said from the top of the stairs.

Mrs Gadny was bawling. 'Stop it,' Thelma shouted.

Henry went down to the hall. 'Come upstairs with me. Come back to bed.'

'She must have wakened the street with her noise.'

Edna opened her bedroom door.

'She's woken Edna, Henry. Is young Michael asleep, Edna?'

'Yes. Has she wet the bed again?'

'I'll go and see.'

Thelma followed Mrs Gadny and Henry into the room.

'What have you been doing? Photographs on your bed at this time of night.'

Mrs Gadny continued sobbing.

Thelma slapped her face. 'Stop it!'

Mrs Gadny made a choking sound.

'My knee. The pain under my knee.'

'Is that why you're bawling?'

'Shut up.'

'Listen, Henry. Listen.'

This was the world she remained in: a world of enemies.

Henry. Thelma. Edna.

'And now Michael.'

'What about Michael?'

'Now him.'

'You've stopped your bawling. We have that to be thankful for.'

All separate.

'Do you love Thelma, Henry?'

'The cheek. The nerve. Listen to her.'

'Mother—' Henry began.

'I am not your mother.'

'No, she isn't.'

'Dear—', he started again.

Everyone called her 'dear'. Thelma did, Henry did, so did the dwarf. Another word to them, without meaning.

'Dear—'

And Mrs Nutley hadn't asked permission to call her 'Faith'.

'Dear—'

'Henry, stop "dear"-ing her and say what you intend saying.'

He pulled his shoulders back and said 'I shall have to find a Home for you to go to. A place where you'll meet people of your own age. I shall make inquiries.'

Henry's belly stuck out. At seventy, it would stick out further.

'It won't be *any* Home. I shall choose it carefully. I shall do my best for you.'

For seven-and-a-half weeks – it *was* seven-and-a-half; she would check with her diary – she had dragged her body about this house. The only suitable description. You could hardly say it was living.

In Roselea. What a ridiculous name. The only roses in sight were those in the sitting-room. The lounge.

'I shall help you choose it, too.'

'No, Thelma. I shall do this on my own.'

Part Three

Nurse Barrow entered with a tray.

'Are you awake?'

White walls.

'Yes.'

'You look rested.'

'Yes.'

'Shall I put the tray on the bed? Or will you eat at table?'

A choice.

'At table.'

'At table?'

'Yes.'

'Raise yourself, then. Do you want to go somewhere first?'

Yes?

'No.'

'I always want to go as soon as I'm awake.'

'The bowl—'

—was dirty. The water wasn't clear because of it. Impossible
to see the faces—

'Which bowl?'

'The toilet,' she snapped. 'I meant to tell you last night. A
drop of bleach would remove the nasty stain.'

'I'll see to it.'

'It isn't pleasant.'

Either.

'No. Come to the table. You're warm enough in your night-dress.'

Thoroughly washed since the flooding.

—Throw it out. With my sheets.

—No. It'll wash.

Two Christmasses back.

'I should have said last night.'

'Eat your eggs.'

Nurse Barrow watched her eat.

'Have they missed me?'

'The ladies?'

—Ladies!

'Ladies! Have they missed me?'

'Oh, yes. They talked about you all of yesterday. They were pleased to hear that you have been given a room of your own. For your sake, they were pleased.'

'I shan't see Mrs Capes. Or those others.'

'Don't stare. Eat. Drink your tea.'

'Yes.'

'The mattress hard enough for you?'

Not 'yes' again. 'Perfect.'

She finished her breakfast. She looked at the nurse and asked: 'Have you a daughter?'

'I should hope not. I haven't a husband.'

'Oh.'

'Though at one time I nearly had. I had a nice young man.'

'Oh.'

'He was a sailor.'

'I had a daughter.'

'A merchant seaman.'

'Celia.'

Nurse Barrow laughed. 'My face now – who'd have me? Hairs come up on my chin. Three times a year I take the scissors to them.'

Queenie Crane's arthritis was having its monthly airing. In a short while, Miss Trimmer thought, we shall hear the latest reports on Nell's back-ache and Alice's water.

Miss Trimmer, anxious that the girls should have a laugh, interrupted Mrs Crane's flow. 'Why don't we take a bet?'

'What on?'

'You said, Queenie, that winter'll soon be with us—'

'Yes, I did. I said we'll all be stuck inside, shivering—'

'Well, let's bet on which of us the cold kills off first.'

'Edie!'

'Who d'you reckon will go? Old Burns? Winnie Hibbs?'

'Winnie Hibbs is going to live for ever,' said Mrs Temple.

'What about us? How are our tickers?'

'Mine's first-class,' said Mrs Crane, 'according to Doctor Gettrup. She felt my titties for lumps this morning.'

'She find any?'

'Of course she didn't. I'm in good condition. Apart, that is, from my arthritis.'

'Yes, Queenie, so you've said. And Alice?'

'My only trouble's my water. Otherwise I'm all right. But you never know what's happening inside you, do you?'

'That's a truth. Alice.'

'Your mind, Edie, your mind.'

'Do we all think Capes'll see the winter through?'

'I can't imagine her passing yet.'

'Why not?'

'I can't. She's too lively.'

'And Dotty Faith, as you call her?'

'Dotty Faith!'

'She might. Except they do say the nervy ones last longest.'

'Yes. You're right. Who you putting your money on, Queenie?'

'I'll say Maggy. Maggy's food can't do her any good.'

'She's visiting the dentist tomorrow. Nurse Trembath's taking her,' said Mrs Gross.

'She'll lose a new set in no time, Nell. I say Maggy.'

'What a conversation! What a way to talk!'

'Who do you say, Edie?'

'Mrs Gross here. I'll put a shilling each way on her.'

'Me?'

'You. Nelly with the cast-iron belly.'

'Me?'

'You.'

'Why?'

'You're too bleeding good to live. That's why.'

The four women laughed.

*

'I haven't seen you take a scone,' said Nurse Barrow.

'I don't want one.'

'Not with some butter?'

'No.'

'They're lovely with butter. Melt in the mouth.'

'No.'

'All you're saying is "no".'

Mrs Gadny took the cup of tea the nurse handed her.

'You surprise me, not eating. I've seen you make short work of cake.'

Mrs Gadny made no response. Her head was down. 'Shall we talk?'

'Talk?'

'Any topic you choose. Or shall we sit quiet? Are you content to sit quiet?'

'Yes. I am.'

'Then that's what we'll do.'

They sat in silence. They sipped their tea.

Mrs Gadny spoke softly. 'Trash. Waste. I said.'

'What you say?'

'Say? Say?' She practically shouted.

'I caught "waste". You said the word "waste".'

'I said nothing. I told you I was content to sit quiet.'

'That's right.'

'That's right.'

They were silent.

'Celia.'

'I'm not Celia, Mrs Gadny.'

Mrs Gadny looked at her; blinked.

'My Christian name's Susan. Susy's my usual label. You're welcome to call me Susy whenever you wish.'

Mrs Affery told Mrs Capes (she'd have preferred to have told Mrs Gadny) that her dreams were taking her back to the start of her life. Last night she was on Itchy Common, a girl again, hair down to her rump. Mrs Capes should have seen the specimens spread out on the grass: drunks, tramps – dying there round the clock.

'Small wonder you scream so much.'

'I know.'

She hoped the pickle factory wouldn't come to her. And those evenings – there were many of them in the first years of their marriage – when Dan had knocked her from one side of the room to the other.

'Matron was in here a long while.'

'Yes.'

'Did you chat?'

'Yes.'

'The cake's all gone. Did Matron eat it?'

'I did.'

'You did, did you? You wouldn't eat the scones—'

'I don't like scones. I like cakes.'

'I shall know in future.'

In future.

'I like a sponge cake best. I told Matron.'

'And she said?'

'She said she'll ask Cook to make me one.'

'You *are* honoured.'

I am. He slept in the crook of my arm.

'You *are* favoured.'

I am.

'I told her – Matron – about my proper doctor's wife. Mrs Bicknall. Of Painter Street. She makes sponge cakes. She has a flair.'

'Has she?'

'A gift.'

'A gift I don't have.'

'Neither does Matron. She admitted.'

'Aha!'

'I asked Thelma – I said to Matron—'

'Who's Thelma?'

'I was telling you. She's Henry, my stepson's wife.'

'I'm clear now.'

'Yes. I asked Thelma, as I said to Matron, if I could cook some meals for her family. When I stayed in her house. She resented me asking.'

'Resented?'

'Plain jealousy. She knew I'd shame her.'

'You should take it as a compliment.'

'I should.'

*

A rumour had reached Mrs Gross's ears. Had it reached Edie's? Concerning a coloured nurse?

'No.'

'Nurse Perceval told Maggy we might be getting one. She came to see Matron last evening.'

'The nurse?'

'What?'

'He invented steam.'

'Who did?'

'Watt did.'

'You've confused me.'

'She come to see Matron, this nurse.'

'Yes. What I gathered from Maggy is that she's brown rather than coloured.'

'Brown's coloured, Nell.'

'Not in my book. When I refer to someone being coloured, I mean black. Brown's lighter than black.'

'God help us!'

'Take Daisy, that cleaner. The one who wears the trilby. She's black. Maggy says this nurse isn't a bit like her – no marks on her face. What I'm trying to tell you is Matron's going to ask each of us in turn whether we approve. Of her looking after us.'

'Oh.'

'I don't mind, do you?'

'I don't mind. Except she'll most likely have a stinking hide.'

'Oh!'

'Go on – click your tongue. I don't support a colour bar but darkies, whatever you say, have stinking hides. It's in their pores.'

'In their pores!'

'It *is*. Fact of nature.'

'Fact of nature!'

'Are you going to repeat everything I say? Pay attention a minute. When they smell us, Nell, the darkies, it works the other way round for them – they fancy *we* smell high. And so we do, to them. Our pores and theirs are designed different. They think we have stinking hides.'

'They think!'

'You *are* going to repeat everything, I can see. Answer me honestly now – have you ever sat anywhere near a Chinaman?'

'Not that I recall. No.'

'I have. I shan't ever forget it either. I was in a railway carriage. A baking hot day, like during the spell we've been having. I was off to see my cousin Violet who married a bit of money in Purley – we weren't allowed to call her "Vi" after her wedding, which is neither here nor there. There was four of us in the carriage, including a clergyman – all respectable people. Stop laughing. The train drew up at a station and this Chinaman got in.'

'He might have been a Jap.'

'He wasn't. I can tell Chinks and Japs apart if you can't.'

'How?'

'Chinks are yellower. May I finish?'

'Yes.'

'He got into the compartment and sat himself down. He smiled at us all, I remember – a friendly little fellow. But we found it more than we could do to smile back. We shared looks, the four of us, and at the next stop we got out. It was like no other smell I've come across, that Chinaman's. Rotten onions is the nearest to it. It was worse than wind breaking, Nell, because that soon goes.'

'Well?'

'Well, it proves my point. About their hides.'

'Proves nothing. When Matron asks me, I shall say I have no objection.'

'I shall think it over.'

Not even Nurse Barrow, not even the wireless, could stop Thelma in full spate.

Henry wasn't her son, was he? If she stopped pitying herself for one minute, she'd perhaps ask herself where his duty lay. It lay with his family. His family wasn't Mrs Faith Gadny, it was Mrs Thelma Gadny.

—Mrs Henry Gadny, Thelma. It would be Mrs Thelma Gadny if you were a widow.

—You'd correct God Almighty, you would.

—Don't blaspheme.

'What's on your mind?'

'Nothing.'

'You're tapping the arm of the chair again.'

So she was.

'So I am.'

'When we return from our walk tonight, Faith; when you've had your bath and done what you've had to; when you're in bed—'

'Yes?'

'Would you like me to read to you?'

'Read?'

'A story. Out of a book.'

'Yes.'

'You don't sound sure.'

'Yes.' She made her voice louder. 'Yes.'

'I can't promise I'll read well.'

She looked at the nurse. Blue eyes. A wart with hairs. The nurse smiled. Grey teeth.

'Don't stare.'

'No.'

'Is it too lonely for you up here?'

'No.'

'You don't miss the ladies?'

'No.'

'I'll find something to read to you tonight.'

Tomorrow, Mrs Capes thought, I shall be in Southend with *them*. A place like Southend will encourage their worst behaviour.

She wasn't averse to a joke, oh no, but not in public. Loud laughter and dirty words were all right between four walls.

She would attach herself to Matron and Mr Green, the curate. She didn't want strangers to see her in a group of common old women. She'd been in service like they had, she wasn't ashamed of it, but with *them* it showed.

'It's a magazine.'

'No.'

'"Her Heart's Awakening". Doesn't that sound tempting? It looks a lovely story.'

'No.'

Jane Eyre was a good book. So was the one about Pip. And *The Pilgrim's Progress* with Ramon Navarro.

—A pile of old-fashioned stories. He won't ever read them.

'No.'

In a dustbin by now. Among food scraps, chocolate boxes, waste. If I tried to read would I reach the end of a line? Would my brain desert me halfway?

'Drink your cocoa.'

Would I forget who did what? Who said what?

'No.'

'You lap up cocoa.'

'Yes.'

The voices would come, pestering. The words wouldn't register. They'd jumble, scatter.

'Drink.'

Let the white walls stay in place. Nurse Barrow by the bed. Don't let my eyes mist.

'While it's hot.'

A room on the top floor.

'I shall have to find a book.'

'*Jane Eyre.*'

'I saw a film of it.'

St John was on his island.

'Just a drop left in the bottom.'

The two women by the pond, the nurse had said, were prostitutes. They lit cigarettes as signs for their customers.

'Shocking. Those women.'

'I quite agree. No respect for their bodies.'

'Shocking.'

'I blame the men. They're to blame.' The nurses looked almost as fierce as the woman who made the noise eating. Not the creature, the other one.

'Did you ever own a cat?' Nurse Barrow asked suddenly.

'Yes. A white one. It died at seventeen.'

'I could tell.' The nurse smiled down. 'An occupation of mine. I look at people and I work out in my mind if they have cat faces or dog faces. You've a cat one.'

'Have I?'

'Your eyes told me. People who have deep eyes, eyes that seem to look inside – they keep cats. A dog face is more open; the eyes are lively. You follow?'

'Yes.'

The nurse kissed her forehead.

*

'A shame she can't come with us.'

'I call it a blessing.'

'To enjoy the sea air.'

'Be quiet, Nell. It's her own fault she's not coming. Give me your nose a minute. I'll squeeze those nasty blackheads out for you.'

'Thank you.'

'Stand still. If you rinsed your face properly, you wouldn't get these.'

'I can't help them. Water's bad for my skin.'

'I won't argue.'

She sat by the window.

'Where shall we go today? With the sun shining we can't stay cooped up in here. It's a crime, love, not to take the best advantage of the weather. Where could we go? Box Hill? The zoo's a thought. Or we could go down the river to Greenwich. Say, Celia. Say.'

No.

'Pecking at your breakfast like a bird you are. Open your mouth, girl, be common, shovel it down. I expect you to grow tall, Celia. To grow you must eat. The golden rule.'

No.

'I didn't sleep last night, Celia. I disturbed your father: he grunted at me. I hope to doze in the sun. In the grass. Like the cat does. I shall lie in the grass and rest. Make my mind up for me, please. You say where it is we're going. Say.'

No.

'Your hair is lovely in this light. It glows, glows…'

'Susy's come.' Nurse Barrow stood beside her. 'Susy's with you.'

'Yes.'

'The Home's so peaceful. Your friends—'

'Friends? Friends?'

'Calm yourself. I meant the ladies. They've gone to the seaside. What a palaver there was before the coach left! Chattering away, rushing around. They've dressed themselves up, put on powder and rouge – you'd have smiled to see them.'

'Is that my tea?'

'I *am* wicked, holding on to it. Here you are.'

'Where's my breakfast?'

'You'll eat in the dining-hall.'

'Oh.'

'The ideal day for the outing, I must say. It will brighten their lives up a bit, give them something to talk about during the winter. Can you picture them, Faith, on the promenade?'

'Yes. I can.'

'Only six of us left in the Home. There's you and me and Cook, and there's Nurse Perceval to see to Mrs Hibbs and Miss Burns. As I said, we'll have the dining-hall to ourselves, and after we've eaten we can spread out in the sun and feel the benefit.'

'In the grass.'

'Little of that out the back. A bench will have to do.'

'Yes.'

'Don't you want the tea?'

'Yes.'

Mrs Gadny drank her tea in two gulps.

'Where's it gone?'

Instead of answering, she complained of a headache.

'Move away from the window.'

Mrs Gadny stood up. She walked across the room and stopped at the door.

'You shall have a tablet,' Nurse Barrow said. 'Are you ready to go down?'

'Yes.'

'You can't go down in only a slip. Find a dress.'

Her dress was on the bed. She held it up.

'No, Faith, not the wool. Not in the heat. Put your print on.'

'Where?' She felt helpless; too weary to look. 'Where?'

'Calm yourself. I can see it hanging with your other clothes.' Nurse Barrow took the orange print from its hanger. 'I'll help you. Stick your head in.'

She lowered her head. Nurse Barrow pulled the dress down her body. 'Shall I comb your hair?'

'My head aches.'

'I'll comb it for you when the pain's cleared.'

'Yes.'

*

A breeze stirred the leaves above them.

'The peace,' Nurse Barrow said. 'The peace.'

No babble of voices by the graves. No stones grinning.

Thelma's heels clicked along the path, then stopped.

'The peace,' said Mrs Gadny.

This morning, staring into the water, the brown stain removed, she'd prayed for Celia's cough to come. She'd called to her – her last call, she knew, rising to a shriek so that the nurse got alarmed, rushed in, hugged her.

—My stay in that house.

—You're sweating. I'll dab your face. Come to the sink.

'You don't call me "dear", Nurse Barrow.'

'I will if you want me to.'

'I'm grateful you don't.'

'What a funny thing to say!'

'It isn't. Not as far as I'm concerned it isn't.'

'You *are* a mystery.'

'Am I?'

You must be, Faith Gadny. You are scarcely understood.

'Am I?'

'Have I set you worrying?'

'No.'

'You're no more a mystery, I suppose, than any other person is. Consider Mrs Affery.'

'With the fur?'

'Yes. Can you make her out?'

'She's simple. A simple creature.'

—If you ask me...

'Poor old Maggy! She's always laughed at. They laugh at me, Faith – have you heard them?'

'No.'

'At my walk.'

'Do they?'

'My mother used to say I walked like a fairy elephant.'

'Did she?'

'Yes.'

They'd eaten a pleasant meal in the big dining-hall. Four of them at the trestle table. Cook wasn't Ada, nothing near, but her chicken fricassee had gone down nicely, settling light. There'd been mushrooms and potatoes cooked with mint and served with butter.

'I enjoyed my food.'

'I saw.'

'Every bit.'

'This is between you, me and the gate-post but it's my opinion that Cook only bothers with the food when she's catering for a small number. Like today. Or when she does for the board – you should see what she does for the board! Most of the time, though, she throws anything on to the plates. Any muck. It brings on ulcers, I swear, just to look at some of her concoctions.'

'It does.'

'No word of what I've just said to Matron—'

'No.'

The church clock struck the hour.

'But I liked my food today.'

'I saw.'

They sat in the kitchen. Red lights, green lights, switches, dials.

—Maurice will carve.

Beef on a plate.

'No.'

'No?'

'Nothing.'

—Tough, Marjorie.

—Tough?

Each time he spoke, Mr Nutley appeared to swallow his teeth.

—Tough, Marjorie.

'I had a meal before I came here, Nurse, that was absolutely disgusting.'

'At your son's?'

'Stepson's. No. At his wife's mother's. At her luxury home in Barnet. My stomach took days to repair.'

'Was it so bad?'

Mrs Gadny looked in all directions. She whispered, 'I was in and out of the lavatory—'

'I meant the meal. Was the meal so bad?'

Mrs Gadny smiled. 'Worse than you could imagine. Her potatoes were out of a packet. Wet lumps.'

'Were they?'

'And the beef! The beef was as tough as a boot.'

'Cook's is sometimes.'

'Not tough like hers that Sunday. My pieces were curling

up on my plate. My wrists ached, I had to work my knife so much.'

'Were you embarrassed?'

'I was. My knife would keep crashing on to the plate and there was Mrs Nutley smiling, smiling.'

'She's your stepson's wife's mother—'

'She is. Blue hair. Powder and paint.'

'One of those.'

'As you say. There she was smiling while I struggled with my beef. I feared for my teeth, Nurse—'

'Doctor Gettrup was very impressed with them, Faith.'

'She said she was amazed. When she found how many were real.'

'She was.'

'Mrs Nutley said I'd look prettier with false.'

'Silly woman.'

'She *is* a silly woman, Nurse. I thought so when I met her. I was never pretty, anyway, even when young. I was plain.'

'You couldn't have been plainer than me.'

'No.' She should have said: Yes, I was. Yes, I was.

'You're not a flatterer.'

'No.'

'Your Celia was pretty?'

'No. She was plain.' She thought she sounded drunk. She'd been drunk once, during the victory celebrations – the truth had poured out of her. This was the truth: 'Celia was plain. If she hadn't been, she might have left her mother; she might have married.'

'I see.'

'If she'd been a beauty she might not have loved her mother so much; she wouldn't have depended—'

'You can't really say.'

'No.'

'A person's nature's what counts.'

'Yes, Nurse.'

'She was sweet-natured?'

'Yes, Nurse.'

Oh, yes. Yes, indeed. Tom said he had an angel for a daughter. She was a loving child – head on her father's knee, against her mother's cheek. Her hair caught the light as she bent over her book.

Glowing.

'Lost.'

'What is?'

'Nothing.'

Tom watched the fire, sighed, drank his beer. Celia in bed, Henry out of the room, he took her hand, pressed it. Certain nights, he told her, the guns went in his head – akk, akk: he made the noises from the back of his throat. Looking down, she saw the blue bulges on his hands. She raised them to her lips.

—Kiss my palms for a change.

—Turn them round.

Good faces were blown away, he said on one occasion. Blood spurted. Feet sank into mud. After the guns and shells a wailing went up.

That one occasion, his face as white as his last night in the hospital, his mouth at her breast, he said into her jumper:

—Ease me.

—How? His hair between her teeth. How?

—Undo the buttons.

The top one wouldn't budge; some loose strand of cotton. She opened the slit in his pants. There was a moment of trouble taking it out.

Then it rose. She remembered to be gentle with the skin at the tip; pulled it back slowly. She heard him say:

—My darling.

So she gripped it firmly. She looked at his small bald patch.

—Love. Love.

It stopped growing. It throbbed.

—Oh, love.

He jerked and let out a moan and the warm cream was on her fingers.

When it was over, fingers sticking together, she realized what she had done. She feared he would weep and add to her embarrassment.

But he moved back into the sofa.

—We must wash ourselves. You, your hands; me, my–my—

—Yes.

'My husband was a great one for his Bible.'

'A religious man.'

'He never went into churches. He hated vicars as a race. He said I could go to services if I liked, it was my life, but I only went once a year. On Christmas Eve, for the carols.'

'Watch night.'

'Yes. He wouldn't join me. Us, rather. I took Celia with me. And she never missed her Sunday school.'

'He read his Bible though?'

'Yes, Nurse. He said he liked the stories. Jeremiah. He took to reading it when he was out in Flanders.'

They noticed a good many changes. The change that struck them most was the train on the pier – the first one had been a delight, a bit of the old world. Those chains that had kept you in your seats, those lamps! Getting to the end of the pier now was just like travelling on the tube. Automatic, it was. Electric.

At noon they filled themselves to bursting with cockles, mussels, winkles. (Mrs Capes chose prawns.) They drank stout, bitter, cider, port. (Mrs Capes had a gin with Matron.)

What did they want to do? Matron asked from the top of the table after begging for a little quiet.

They wanted to laze in the sun until tea. There was enough amusement to be had from the sight of the bathers – the bosoms and Burns wobbling past.

Mr Green was going to show Matron the eleventh-century priory – which of the ladies were interested? Mrs Capes definitely was – it was educational. Any other volunteers?

'Not me.'

'No, thanks.'

'Thank you for the invitation, Curate—'

'Yes, thank you for the invitation.'

'I have these ruins to look at, Mr Green, without seeing any more.'

'Edie!... I'll stay with my friends, thank you kindly, Curate.'

Outside the cafe they formed two groups: the priory party to go one way, the beach party the other. Nurse Trembath and Doctor Gettrup said they would take charge of the rebels, whom they led off along the sea front.

Mrs Affery stopped in front of the Ivy House – the bar was filled with husbands in shirt-sleeves, steadily getting plastered. Dan had done a week's hard drinking in that bar on their honeymoon.

'Come on, Maggy.'

Her mouth was sore; her gums itched. She turned her back on the women – who waited a few yards ahead – and took out her replacement teeth. She wrapped them in her nearly clean hanky and dropped them in the carrier-bag she had brought for souvenirs.

'Maggy!'

They were smiling when she joined them.

'Close your eyes,' said Mrs O'Blath, her hands behind her back, 'and promise not to open them.'

Mrs Affery closed her eyes.

'Don't open them till I give the word.'

Mrs Affery felt something on her head.

'Open.'

Mrs O'Blath held on to her knees to stop herself biting the pavement.

'What is it?'

'And she's lost her gnashers!'

'What you put on me?'

'Can't you see, Maggy?' said Mrs Crane. 'A cowboy hat.'

'A stetson, Maggy.'

People walked by slowly, staring and pointing at Mrs O'Blath.

'It has words on it.' Nurse Trembath took Mrs Affery's arm.

'What words?'

'It says "Calamity Jane Novelty Hat".'

In the coach coming back they sang 'If you were the only girl in the world' and 'The Old Bull and Bush'. Mrs O'Blath sang a verse of an Irish song no one had ever heard of in a voice that turned out to be very sweet and true.

Some minutes out of London the coach was stopped for Miss Trimmer. Mrs Gross helped her towards a ditch and held her as she groaned.

'Why'm I plagued with your bloody voice?' she shouted at what was now the ceiling. A second ago Thelma had been there, a hand on her hip, leaning against the doorpost.

The ceiling drifted away. Thelma walked towards her, arms swinging like a soldier's.

'Photograph.'

One, two; one, two.

If I count, she thought, I will stop her speaking. I might even sleep.

'One—'

She swallowed the drop of water that fell into her mouth. It had a salty taste. Before she could continue, Thelma had taken over the counting.

—Two. Three. Four.

Photos were the answer. Plus concentration. Tom said to Henry that concentration and perseverance were the tests of a man's character. Some boys with slow brains were known to achieve wonders later in their lives simply because they had forced themselves to persevere.

She would concentrate on the photos as soon as she had the energy to step out of bed.

Tom said it was no use – that boy had willed himself not to listen. Henry made contact with no one.

—I wanted to see the boy cry. When I tanned him.

Instead of appearing for his meals and sitting by and going to his room. A visitor to the house.

—All he is. A visitor. Not a son to me.

Eyes small as a pig's.

—Do as you please, boy, as you will. You do right to leave. Let me finish my beer in peace.

Thelma slammed her book shut.

—He owes you nothing.

—If you wish to insult me, Thelma, insult me when your mouth's empty.

—How have you thanked him? You've made his home a place of misery—

—You read too many rotten books. A place of misery!

—Christ!

—You shouldn't blaspheme, even if you don't—

—Is it four o'clock? Grant me strength if it isn't.

Any photograph. This, that or the other. Tom or Celia, even herself, Mrs Barber or her Rose. Any photograph would do the trick so long as there was a face on it.

She dragged her special case from under the bed. She opened it. Her choice underwear, yes. Tom's Bible, yes, which she hadn't the heart to open and read. Lavender in its bag.

'They're under my cap.'

But, she discovered, they weren't.

'Think.'

The pieces fell to her feet. She stood up. More pieces fell. A pile formed.

'No.'

She'd laughed. She'd been serenely happy. The one called Capes and the nurse without the hairs had drawn back from her. The sky outside the ward was purple. She'd managed, that beautiful evening, to keep their hands off. Their hands could come this minute, she thought, and smother me and I'd be just as happy. The pain she felt when she heard the cough was pleasant compared to the pain that came with Thelma's words. The weeks at Roselea were weeks in the wilderness. She'd faced pettiness every single day. She'd tried to accustom herself to a loveless existence. To think of that awful time was worse than the sight of Celia above the sheets. That house had brought her down. She'd gone into it with some opinion of herself. She left it a thing, waste to be disposed of; the barometer at Fine.

It was this room that was the cause. Downstairs, with Capes and the creature and the staring woman, her mind hadn't been bothered. Downstairs, she had only thought about Tom and Celia. Not her and him and old Granny Grunt from the corner of the Terrace and that dreadful pair in the luxury factory.

She wanted Nurse Susy to kiss her to sleep again, to laugh as the hairs tickled her cheek.

'All was well until nine at night, Matron,' said Nurse Barrow. 'Cook gave us a delicious chicken fricassee and Mrs Gadny ate her plate bare. In the afternoon, as it was still hot, we went out into the grounds – the two of us – and we sat on a bench together and soaked in the sunshine. And there we stayed for hours. We chatted away merrily. It was a surprise to me, the way she talked. She usually just mutters.'

'She does. Tell me what she talked about.'

'Her husband. But her daughter mostly. She must have told me everything about her, Matron, from cradle to grave. I know what colour her eyes were, when her wisdom teeth were removed, how good she was about the home – I feel I must know her inside out. After tea, which we took late, she muttered a bit – different names came up. I had to strain to catch them.'

'And at nine?'

'Tears, Matron. An ocean this time. We were out in the grounds until after eight struck; then the wind got up and we both started to shiver. So I brought her in and took her to the lounge to watch the TV. She sat quite content for some while – she said that the daffs need a clean – and she seemed, whenever I looked at her, to be enjoying the programme. At five past nine she screamed. I nearly jumped out of my skin. I asked her what the scream was for: had it been the play we were looking at? It wouldn't have surprised me, I felt like screaming myself. No, it wasn't the play. She grunted like some animal, Matron.'

'Grunted?'

'Grunted.'

'Goodness!'

'She cried the rest of the evening. I put her to bed and she stopped. She asked me to kiss her good night, which I did, and then she turned on her side and was dead to the world in a minute.'

'Poor Nurse Barrow.'

'Not poor me, Matron. Poor *her*. I must say I feel rather attached to her.'

'Do you? That's encouraging. With your help, she still might settle. We'll get her out of the room, shall we?'

'Not yet—'

'No, no. By degrees. I want her to attend Mrs Hibbs's party. I'll arrange with the ladies to treat her gently. We'll see whether she can behave herself. I hope this is a simple case of depression, nothing more.'

'I hope so.'

'And that she'll learn to be happy. As the others have.'

'I hope so.'

'Mrs Capes was a bad case when she first came.'

'So I was told.'

'In a different way. She was irritable, short-tempered. And with more cause than Mrs Gadny. Mrs Gadny's daughter died but Mrs Capes's son took his life.'

'I never knew.'

'Gas.'

'How frightful… I'll try to be nicer to her than I have been, Matron.'

'Yes.'

'Did you enjoy your day at the seaside, Matron?'

'Yes. Yes, I did. I have to confess that I escaped from my old trouts for a good two hours.' Matron smiled, shut the smile off quickly. 'You should have heard them singing in the coach. I turned round and looked at them once and I almost cried. You wouldn't believe that pack could seem so innocent. And Miss Trimmer had just been sick!'

'I heard.'

'I pulled myself together, Nurse. I told myself off for being sentimental.'

Mrs Gadny laughed. Fancy thinking she could draw! The lines she'd made on her writing-pad were a baby's squiggles. According to Tom, a grown-up person was one who knew his limitations. Fancy thinking she could draw Celia's face!

Mrs Crabbe was very surprised when she read the letter of resignation. She called her into the pink dressing-room.

—Your spelling, Faith, is remarkable. Walter is for ever complaining about mine. He read your letter and he said 'She spells better than you, my precious, and she wasn't even educated!'

Letters were one thing, drawings another.

'I suggest, Edith, that you don't feed yourself so well today. I'd hate to see you have another accident.'

'The cow,' Miss Trimmer said to Mrs Gross as Mrs Capes went into the Home.

'You deserved it.'

'You're a loyal friend, aren't you? Why did I deserve it?'

'Goading her about Mrs Gadny. Carrying on. Can't you tell when your remarks hit home?'

'She told Moaning Minnie she was simple, didn't she?'

'Nevertheless, Edith, she misses her. Mrs Capes wanted her for a friend.'

'A friend!'

'She's never been fond of any of us, has she? Mrs Gadny is more her kind of person.'

'They're welcome to each other.'

'You should guard your tongue.'

'Should I? Should I?'

'You're petulant now. It hurts you – doesn't it? – being put in your place. You've gone like a girl.'

*

The fireplace was about where this bed is.

On the mantelpiece were Tom's pipes and the tin for his tobacco (they remained in their usual places after his death), the seashell, the black wooden elephant whose tusks had gone. That was all there was on the mantelpiece. In front of the fireplace were a brass fender, a brass coalscuttle with brass tongs and, in the summer, an iron vase she filled with flowers.

It was tiring work, seeing the house piece by piece. Why hadn't a picture of each room stayed with her?

'I *am* old.'

These struggles.

'Old.'

She began to cry. Her stick tapped on the cobbles; she shuffled and stumbled. Children shouted names.

'Go.'

The door closed behind her and the noise ended. She sniffed. The doctor said:

—Disinfectant.

The doctor asked her to remove her clothes.

Eventually, she was naked.

She couldn't look at her poor body. Her breasts had always been too small. Tom, inside her, tongue at her eyelids, said:

—Doll, Doll.

And later, dying, his face cleared of lines (except for his scar; you couldn't expect that to be wiped away), he called her 'Doll'. He meant Dolores.

'Faith, love.'

He blinked. He smiled.

—Faith. Yes.

Dolores, she would have told him if he hadn't been so weak, was dead these thirty years. Henry was with her when it happened. The boy stood at the foot of her bed and watched. She was bearing somebody's child.

His saying 'Doll' proved she was in his thoughts. The size of oranges.

This room. These white walls.

—The effect on his young mind, Mrs Barber said, seeing his mother go. It must have left its mark.

Flies round the light-shade. In the ward they stuck to the strip of gum.

'No one cares if they annoy me.'

They were fatter, heavier flies. Their buzzing was louder.

'Driving me wild.'

In a month they would start to die. Did they fall to the ground, their legs in the air? Did they burst?

—Doll.

Of course he was thinking of her. He was thinking of her body.

'Not me.'

Thirty years after. Her flesh. Her smell.

Nurse Barrow said, 'Faith, let me help you to dress. It's time for our walk.'

'Help me.'

'I will.'

'These flies.'

'Buggers, aren't they? Your knickers first. Don't cry, sweetheart.'

Mrs Gadny's head was down.

'Look at yourself,' Nurse Barrow said.

Mrs Gadny looked into the mirror.

'I think some powder, don't you? As it's a party.'

Mrs Gadny nodded.

'A dab on each, dear. Oh dear, I mustn't say "dear", must I?' The nurse laughed. 'It's forbidden.'

Mrs Gadny said 'Yes.'

Nurse Trembath entered the room. 'I say, we *do* look glamorous.'

'Don't we?' said Nurse Barrow.

'In our smart party dress.'

'Isn't it smart?'

'And our hair nicely combed!'

Mrs Gadny looked at the floor.

'Take a last peep before we go, Faith.'

Mrs Hibbs slept, her head dangling and her mouth open, oblivious of the table that had been laid with food and drink, and the streamers that hung from the ceiling. Miss Burns sat upright in her bed, pillows at her back for support.

Miss Trimmer pushed the door open. The women followed her into the ward.

'What a show!' said Mrs Gross.

'My! My!'

'All this for Winnie!' said Mrs Crane.

There were long-stemmed roses in a silver bowl in the centre of the table. The large birthday cake had nine candles. Someone had arranged the telegrams and cards around it. Mrs Gross thought it had been beautifully done.

'A bottle of port,' said Mrs Temple.

Mrs Capes was pleased they'd supplied both kinds of sherry.

When Mrs Affery said 'All this for Winnie!' the women turned to look at Mrs Hibbs. She slept as usual, in her usual position; a frightening reminder.

Mrs Gross asked in her quietest voice: 'Have they washed her?'

'Why whisper? She won't hear.'

'Do you think, Edie, that they've washed her today?'

'Go and smell.'

'I couldn't do that.'

'See if they've washed her, Maggy. Go and sniff.'

Mrs Affery put her nose to Mrs Hibbs's cheek. 'She smells of lavender.'

'Lavender!'

'They've polished her!'

'Lavender!'

'Are her teeth in, Maggy?' asked Mrs O'Blath.

Mrs Affery bent a little lower. 'I can't make out.'

'Tell her a joke,' said Miss Trimmer. 'Make her smile.'

Mrs Capes was the only one not to laugh.

'Her hair smells fresh.'

'They *have* been thorough.'

Mrs Hibbs stirred in her sleep.

'She's moving!'

Miss Trimmer suggested they take their places, seeing as how the birthday girl was still alive. 'Who' – she paused before finishing her question – 'is sitting where?'

'Matron will be at the top, won't she?'

'In that case, Nell, we'll sit at *this* end.'

They saw, as soon as they were seated, that there was a vacant chair between Mrs Crane and Mrs Affery.

'Where's Dotty Faith?'

'She'll sit next to you, Queenie.'

'No, she won't. Maggy, move one up.'

'What for?'

'I don't want *her* next to me. Especially if she gets the weeps.'

'Nurse Barrow says she's quite cheerful.'

'Please, Maggy. Please move.'

'Lot of fuss.'

'Thanks, Maggy dear.'

'Lot of fuss.'

'Now she's next to me,' Mrs Temple complained. 'I don't want to have to suffer her.'

Mrs Capes hit the table with her fist. The glasses tinkled, the jellies wobbled, two cards fell flat. 'Why you're being so choosy all of a sudden I don't know. You speak as though Mrs Gadny's an insect or something.'

'Someone I know said she was simple,' Miss Trimmer interrupted.

'Someone you know regrets she ever said it, Edith Trimmer.'

'That's why someone's stopped smiling lately, is it?'

'Answer your own questions. Move your fine bottom, Alice Temple. Change seats with me.'

'I didn't—'

'Get up! Come over here where it's safe. I'd hate to see a lady like yourself catching a disease from Mrs Gadny. Come on.'

Mrs Temple looked to her friends for support. Mrs Gross smiled in her direction and pointed to the chair Mrs Capes had now vacated.

Mrs Temple got up, moved slowly round the table. Passing Mrs Capes, she began: 'I didn't—'

'You did.'

Mrs Capes sat down. She clasped her hands together to stop them shaking.

'Lot of fuss,' said Mrs Affery.

'Yes, Maggy.'

'Somebody's coming.'

They listened. Nurse Trembath was saying, 'They can't wait for the party to begin.'

Mrs O'Blath placed the cards back in position.

Then the door opened. Mrs Gadny stood between Nurse Barrow and Nurse Trembath. The nurses said 'Good afternoon, ladies.'

'Good afternoon.'

'Good afternoon, Nurse Trembath.'

'Good afternoon, Nurse Barrow.'

'They can't wait for the party to begin.'

'We've brought Mrs Gadny to the party,' Nurse Barrow said.

Mrs Gross said, 'Hullo, Faith.'

'Say "Hullo".'

'Hullo.'

Mrs Gross said, 'We've saved a place for you.'

'She's been looking forward to the party all week.'

'So have we.'

'Is that Mrs Gadny's place, Mrs Affery?'

'Yes, Nurse.'

'Come and sit down, dear.'

The nurses led Mrs Gadny to her chair.

'Good afternoon, Faith.'

'Say "Good afternoon" to Mrs Capes.'

'Good afternoon.'

'Are you happy in your room, Faith?'

'Yes.'

'I'm so glad.'

Miss Trimmer's voice broke in. 'We were saying before you came in, Nurse Trembath, how nice Mrs Hibbs looks.'

'She's been smartened up for today.'

'Will she eat and drink?'

'She'll have a sip of sherry. Cake would lie heavy on her.'

'You ladies,' said Nurse Barrow, 'will have the pleasure of the cake. Poor Mrs Hibbs will eat junket.'

'What about Miss Burns? Will she have sherry?'

'A sip, I expect.'

'She'll get drunk and roll her eyes.'

Mrs Crane and Mrs O'Blath giggled. Nurse Barrow smiled. 'Don't be cruel, Edith.'

'No offence meant.'

'Are your teeth in, Mrs Affery?'

'Yes, Nurse.' Mrs Affery displayed them.

'You must keep them in for the party. Matron's instructions.'

'Yes, Nurse.'

'Otherwise there'll be trouble.'

'Yes, Nurse.'

'Isn't it wonderful?' – Nurse Trembath thought the women needed their spirits lifting – 'Mrs Hibbs reaching ninety?'

'Oh, yes.'

'Yes.'

'Yes.'

'I shan't get to that age.' Miss Trimmer sounded very certain. 'I'd sooner be boxed than be in the state she is.'

'How morbid of you, Miss Trimmer. Today's a happy day. Nurse Barrow and me won't have you saying such things.'

'Yes, Edith, stop it.'

'It's sense.'

'Edie!'

Matron appeared with Nurse Perceval, who carried a tray on which were two bowls of junket.

'Good afternoon, Matron.'

'Good afternoon. Is everyone present?'

'We're all here, Matron,' Nurse Barrow answered.

Matron stood at the head of the table. 'Wake Mrs Hibbs, Nurse Perceval.'

'Yes, Matron.' The nurse left one of the bowls on Miss Burns's locker, carried the other to Mrs Hibbs.

Nurse Perceval shook Mrs Hibbs gently. Mrs Hibbs's mouth snapped shut; her eyes opened.

'Lift her head up. Let her see us.'

The nurse pushed Mrs Hibbs's chin up. She removed her hand, waited for the head to slump forward. It stayed upright. Mrs Hibbs stared at the table.

'Happy birthday, Mrs Hibbs,' said Matron.

'Happy birthday, Mrs Hibbs.'

'Before we propose the toast, we must decide what you ladies will be drinking. Raise your hands, those who would like dry sherry.'

Mrs Capes and the nurses raised their hands.

'Now those who would prefer sweet.'

Mrs Affery, Mrs Gross and Mrs Temple raised their hands.

'The rest of you, I presume, will drink the port?'

'Yes, Matron.'

'And you, Mrs Gadny?... Mrs Gadny?'

'Sherry or port, Faith?' Nurse Barrow asked.

'Port.'

'Port please, Matron.'

'Shall we do the honours, Nurses? And then we can cope with the cake.'

The nurses poured the drinks.

'Not too much, Nurse.'

'No more than a drop for me.'

'Fill Edie's right up.'

Nurse Perceval poured Mrs Hibbs a small sweet sherry; Nurse Trembath did the same for Miss Burns.

'Can we manage to carry the cake to Mrs Hibbs, Nurse Perceval?'

'We can try, Matron.'

'Heave ho!'

The women laughed.

'Place it by her on the bed.'

'Easy does it.'

'Put the knife in her hand. It will be nice for her to cut the cake.'

The hand shook violently.

'Hold her firmly.'

'I can't manage her.'

'Try to cut the cake.'

Nurse Perceval lifted the hand in the direction of the cake.

'It's impossible, Matron.'

'Very well. Let's return it to the table.'

Miss Trimmer said 'Heave ho!' this time.

'Aren't you going to light the candles?'

'I almost forgot, Mrs Affery.' Matron lit the candles. 'Since you reminded me, my dear, you must blow them out.'

'Yes, go on, Maggy.'

'Go and have a puff, Maggy.'

'You must take a deep, deep breath.'

'Come along, Mrs Affery.'

'Yes, Matron.'

Mrs Affery leaned over the cake. She breathed in deeply; blew. Four candles went out. Mrs O'Blath's laughter disposed of the rest.

'Thank you,' Matron said. 'Both of you.'

Mrs Affery sat down. She glared at Mrs O'Blath. Nurse Barrow said, 'Don't drink yet, Miss Trimmer. Wait for the toast.'

The pieces of cake were passed down the table.

'What lovely cake!'

'Such icing!'

'And marzipan.'

'It looks very rich.'

'Has everyone her cake?'

'Yes, thank you, Matron.'

'Then it's time for me to propose the toast.'

Mrs Capes clapped. The women stood up. Mrs Gadny, head down, stayed seated. Nurse Barrow helped her out of her chair.

'Raise your glasses, ladies. To Mrs Hibbs, the oldest inhabitant of the Jerusalem Home, a happy birthday. And may she live to be a hundred.'

'A hundred!'

'Yes.'

'Yes.'

'To Mrs Hibbs!'

'To Mrs Hibbs!'

Nurse Perceval nudged Mrs Hibbs, who had fallen asleep.

'Have your birthday sherry, dear.' She put the glass to Mrs Hibbs's mouth, tilted it. A trickle of sherry slid down her throat.

'Is she drinking, Nurse?'

'In fits and starts.'

'And Miss Burns, Nurse Trembath?'

'She's taking a little.'

'Good. Now, ladies, isn't there something we should sing?'

'Sing?'

'Sing, yes. What is it people sing on birthdays?'

'"Happy birthday to you",' said Mrs Affery.

'Of course it is. Shall we all sing?'

The women sang, shakily:

'Happy birthday to you,
Happy birthday to you,
Happy birthday, dear Winnie—'

(Matron sang 'Mrs Hi-ibbs')

'—Happy birthday to you.'

'Thank you. Sit down, all of you.'

Mrs Affery, still standing, stared at Mrs Hibbs. 'She smiled!'

'Who smiled?'

'Mrs Hibbs. She smiled!'

'Did she, Nurse?'

'I think she did.'

'We've made her happy.'

Mrs Affery sat down.

'When she's a hundred,' Mrs Crane asked, 'won't she hear from the Queen?'

'Yes, she will. Her Majesty sends telegrams to all her centenarians. The Mayor and Mayoress sent a very thoughtful message today.'

'Did they, Matron?'

'Shall I read it out?'

'Yes, please.'

'Which one is it? Ah, yes. "Mrs Hibbs, The Jerusalem Home. Greetings on reaching your great age. Mayor and Mayoress Ernest and Sylvia Marsh."'

'It *is* thoughtful.'

'Thoughtful.'

'Thoughtful. As Matron said.'

'The Mayor has promised us a visit this Christmas. He will come to our show. I've told him about your singing, Mrs Capes.'

'Warned him, I hope, Matron.'

'Not at all. You have a charming voice. Hasn't she, ladies?'

'Charming voice.'

'Charming. That's right.'

'Thank you,' said Mrs Capes. 'Thank you.'

'Are we all eating our cake?' Some of the women answered 'Yes'; others, mouths full, nodded.

Nurse Barrow had cut Mrs Gadny's portion into small squares. 'Eat up, Faith. It's not like you not to eat cake.'

'The other ladies – are they coping with their junket?'

'Yes, Matron.'

'Is Mrs Gadny eating?'

'Beginning to.'

Mrs Affery didn't want her icing.

'Where's your sweet tooth?' asked Mrs O'Blath.

'Would you like my icing, Mrs Capes?'

'No, thank you, Maggy.'

Mrs O'Blath went on. 'If you put it under your pillow, you'll dream of the man you're to marry.'

'It's wedding cake you do that with, Clever Dick. You want my icing, Mrs Gadny?'

Nurse Barrow said 'No, thank you.'

'Leave it on your plate.'

'Pity to waste it, Matron.'

'Even so.'

'Wake up, Winnie. Finish your junket.'

Mrs Gadny said 'Not here.'

'Sh, Faith. If you can't eat, sip your port.'

'No.'

'Sh! Sh!'

'Celia.'

'Her and her bloody Celia.'

'Now then, Edith. Sip your port, Faith.'

'Fill the ladies' glasses, Nurse Trembath, when you've attended to Miss Burns.'

'Yes, Matron.'

'Thank you, Matron.'

'Not here.'

'Who's not here?'

'Celia's not here, Edie,' said Mrs Crane.

'She's at her harp. Or burning.'

'Be quiet!' Nurse Barrow shouted.

'Miserable bloody face making people bloody miserable—'

'Mrs Crane, be quiet please,' Matron ordered.

'Face like death about the place,' Miss Trimmer resumed.

'Winnie looks happier than she does,' Mrs Temple added.

'And she can't barely hear or see—'

'Ladies! Show some consideration. Remember that this is a party.'

Silence.

Mrs Gadny looked at the black hole as it widened. She blinked. Old women's faces. Nothing but.

'No.'

Mouths opened.

'No.'

One mouth. One black hole. Its warm air drawing her in.

Mrs Gadny screamed.

She would have to use her hands. She would have to fight her way out.

'Watch it!' said Mrs Affery, avoiding the claw that came towards her.

The dark cleared. Yellow violets changed into red hair. White tiles became sheets, ironed crisp – grey rings above them.

'My God,' said Mrs Capes. 'My God.'

Nurse Barrow pinned Mrs Gadny's hands to her sides. Mrs Gadny groaned.

'Look at her. Mad. Mad.'

'Mad. Mad. She is. Mad.'

'An animal. An animal.'

'Get rid of her.'

'Send her away. Send her to a bin.'

'Bedlam'd do for her.'

'Stay in your places, ladies. Nurse Barrow will attend to her.'

Nurse Barrow maintained her grip. Mrs Gadny's head moved from side to side, her tongue over her lower lip.

'Nurse should smack her face. One good back-hander,' said Mrs O'Blath.

'Stand up, Faith.'

Mrs Gadny allowed Nurse Barrow to lift her.

'Kick her arse.'

'Get rid of her. Throw her out.'

'Spoiling the party.'

'Spoiling the fun.'

'Come now, Faith. We'll go to your room. The two of us. We'll go to your room. Together. We'll go. Come now.'

Nurse Barrow led Mrs Gadny out.

'The day was happy until—'

'Now, now, Mrs Crane. Nurses, pour the sherries and ports.'

The nurses filled the glasses.

'I'll go tiddly.'

'Any more and I'll sing.'

'Careful, I'm not a scarlet woman.'

'Warms you, port.'

'We need a drink after *her*.'

'Shall we all read Mrs Hibbs the verses on the cards we sent her?'

'That's a nice idea, Matron,' said Mrs Capes.

'Who's to begin? Mrs Affery?'

'Can't read. Never could. Or write.'

'Oh, yes. Of course. Shall we go round the table, then? You first, Mrs O'Blath. You read your card.'

'With pleasure, Matron.'

Mrs O'Blath put on her reading glasses; took her card from the group. She rose. She cleared her throat.

'Before you begin, my dear, would you wake Mrs Hibbs, please Nurse?'

Nurse Perceval nudged Mrs Hibbs.

'Right, Mrs O'Blath. Begin.'

Mrs O'Blath cleared her throat a second time. She read slowly, separating each word;

'You who have travelled on Life's troubled way,
Whose hair the years have turned a gentle grey,
Smile your sweet smile this happy, special day,
And drive all cares and worries far away.'

The women clapped enthusiastically.

'Lovely words.'

'It's beautiful.'

'Well chosen, Mrs O'Blath. Are you ready to read, Mrs Temple?'

'Yes, Matron.'

Nurse Perceval spoke into Mrs Hibbs's ear. 'Did you enjoy your poem?'

—A walnut whirl.

The voice coming from the hole.

—A dozen soft centres.

A fur.

Not that face, creature's face. Tom's face:

One brown eye. There! No, two brown eyes. He had a scar, not an eye missing. There! Two eyes and a scar. And wide nostrils. Almost a boxer's nose.

There!

No. No photos.

'Gone.'

Brown eyes, scar, nose—

'Tom.'

The name.

Was she of use because she could cook, sew, run a house? Because she lit the fire, laid out his slippers, poured his beer? Polished his boots so that he looked down at his face?

He only mentioned love the once. Or did he? The night he made her hands go sticky. It was 'Doll' at the end.

'Doll.'

What you come to.

—Tell her.

'What you—'

—The best I could find. I visited several.

—Tell her about the others.

—They had very old people in them.

—Senile, weren't they? Tell her.

—Fossils.

—The Jerusalem's only women, isn't it?

—Yes. Your kind.

'My kind?'

—I'd say so. Will you come and look?

'No.'

—Tomorrow?

'No.'

—Stop playing the martyr.

'Fill in the papers.'

—You must see the place.

'No. Papers.'

—You must…

She had her doubts about Celia. As well as Tom. Celia was for ever collecting at her office; rattling her tin.

You lived for years, you never thought—

She hadn't looked down at her breasts in the house the way she'd done lately. Oh, no. No cause to. The veins were veins. Celia was Celia and Tom was Tom.

And no questions, unless it was the weather, were we winning the war, was it the day for Mrs Barber and her Rose's bath—

Celia pitied anyone and everyone. That was why she stayed in the house. There was strain in her voice that last year, definitely. Her patience was running out.

No doubts before.

Some peace—

When she stood by the door, St John seemed to be looking at her.

Here was the pond. Not the pond on the common, where the two tarts stood, the pond in the park. Ducklings, as it was spring, guarded by their mothers.

—We'll be friends, won't we, Michael?

Nothing.

—The way you snuggled up to me in the car! You let me hold you while you slept.

Nothing.

—Your mother doesn't love you, Michael, she dared to say. I love you, though. I could be a sort of mother to you. I could take you to the zoo. Have you been to the Tower?

Nothing.

—Celia would go with me…

—Her book.

—Her book, yes. Your sister bullies you, Michael, and your mother, your mother…

She had to be careful what she said.

—Give me your hand.

—No.

—No?

—No.

—I'll look after you…

Michael shifted to the end of the bench.

—No! he shouted.

—Oh, Michael.

Michael's eyes widened.

—I'm not crying, Michael. It's the wind. Can't you feel it on your face? It's the wind.

She stood in front of him. She leaned over to kiss him. His fists pummelled her belly; his foot hit her knee.

'Oh, Michael.'

What you come to.

This is what you come to: you live for seventy years and you find one night you're stuck in a room, in a chair, and your body's beneath you, waiting for the chill to strike it, till your eyes see only black and no sound to remind you.

You've memories of rooms and faces and all manner of things but they go as quickly as they come.

How long before she was nothing? Years?

She would sit for years.

If I hurt myself, I'll cry—

She beat against the wall. Her hands and her bare feet met the stone. She dropped exhausted to the floor. Blood flowed from grazes on her knuckles and from a small cut on her right foot.

Her eyes could as well be glass.

Miss Trimmer rushed into the dining-hall, waving an envelope. 'I met the young man in the corridor. Her son.'

'Stepson.' Mrs Capes corrected her.

'Stepson. What do you think he gave me?'

'A kiss.'

'A pat on your bum.'

'A quart of stout.'

'Twins.'

'You are a dirty bitch sometimes, Queenie. You haven't guessed.'

'A bunch of grapes.'

'Flowers.'

'I wouldn't have your memories. What am I shaking in my hand? He gave me the photos.'

'What photos?'

'What he took. When he was here that Sunday.'

'Those photos!'

'Those photos!'

'Yes. Those photos.'

'Show them.'

'Let's see them.'

'Hold yourselves. Hold your horses. He give me eight copies. So there's one for each of us and one to spare. Put your hands out. Here's yours, Queenie.'

'I say! Look at us!'

'Nell.'

'Thank you.'

'Alice.'

'Thanks, Edie. Well!'

'Maggy.'

'Thank you. Oh, dear!'

'Mrs Capes.'

'Thank you, Miss Trimmer.'

'Yours, Peggy.'

'I'm grateful to you, Edie. Good God!'

'Two for me.'

'Look at her! All eyes and gums!'

'You mean me?'

'What a sight!'

Mrs Crane could only make out her nose.

'The best part of your face,' said Miss Trimmer.

'I can't see Mrs Capes in this picture.'

'I was with Mrs Gadny, Mrs Temple. It was while I was friends with her.'

'Doctor Gettrup and the specialist reached the same conclusion.'

'I see.'

'If she responds to treatment, she'll recover.'

'Where is this place?'

'In Kent.'

'I see.'

'It's modern. It has more facilities.'

'I see.'

'The specialist said she must go there as soon as possible. While there's hope.'

'Yes. Very well. I see.'

'You're wise, Mr Gadny... Are you fond of her?'

'No, Matron. I can't say I am. In all honesty. I want to help her, of course. I'm not close to her, Matron.'

'Not the answer I expected.'

'I've learnt to be honest. I thank my father for that.'

'They called it a party, Celia. A party! Pigs at a trough would eat cleaner. Their mouths, love. And *her* mouth, a hole in front of me, I was dizzy, I fell... They're filth, aren't they? Everyone is. We all come to... All there is for any of us... Trash, waste. I said. I said...'

There! The high window. The bed.

'You're white. You're drained. Oh, love.'

Celia coughed.

'Blood's gone from you.'

She sobbed into a pillow. The joy, the relief.

'There, Faith. Susy's with you.'

She looked into the nurse's face. 'I feel so happy.'

'Happy!'

'Yes. I feel so better, Susy.' She smiled. 'My heart's breaking.'

'Is it?

'Yes. Yes.'

'How are your bandages? Tight enough?'

'Yes.'

'You're making Susy's blouse wet.'

'I don't care.'

*

'She won't touch me. I don't want her clammy black paws near me.'

'Why didn't you say so to Matron, Queenie?'

'She would've taken it wrong. She wouldn't have seen my meaning.'

'Coward.'

'I've heard you lot go on about the darkies. But you all said "Yes" to having one look after you—'

'So did you.'

'I'm quite aware. *I* didn't want to disgrace myself. I'm not the only hypocrite—'

'I've no objection to Nurse Wilkins—'

'Maybe you haven't, Nell. What about Edie, though? And Alice? And Mrs Capes?'

'You'll just have to put up with her.'

'I grant you they're no worse than Jews—'

'My husband, Mrs Crane,' said Mrs Gross, 'was a Jew. He bore all the marks. He may not have practised his faith but he was a good husband. He was a good husband.' Mrs Gross rose from the table and walked slowly out of the dining-hall.

'In the country.'

'Not with Mrs Barber, Matron. She's dead.'

'Yes. Not with her. In another Home.'

'I'm happy here. I'm content.'

And she was beaming to prove it.

'You can have a rest. A holiday.'

'A holiday.'

'In the country.'

Nurse Trembath was suddenly firm. 'Miss Trimmer, I must put the screens round her. She has to be washed.'

'Come on, Edie.'

'Poor Peg. Poor Peg.'

'Mrs Gross, ask Cook to brew some tea.'

Miss Trimmer's hands were at her mouth. Her shoulders were heaving.

'Mr Parsdoe from the General will be with us any minute.'

'Edie. Edie.'

'There's bound to be a post-mortem. Go along, Miss Trimmer.'

Miss Trimmer broke away from Mrs Gross. She grasped the rail at the end of Miss Burns's bed. 'Why couldn't you bloody die? You bloody staring great thing.'

'Edie—'

'I'd bloody strangle the thing given half the chance.'

'Take her away, Mrs Gross.'

'Edie, come on—'

'Before I lose my temper.'

'Susy's come… You've dressed!'

'I dressed myself to go. I'm packed.'

'That was clever of you.'

'I powdered my face.'

'So you did.'

'I'd been crying.'

'To cover up.'

'I had to powder. I'm sad at leaving.'

'You'll be back.'

'Yes. You left the door open. I went and washed. I looked down at the bowl.'

'What's the box?'

'Chocolates. Do you want them? I think they've melted.'

'I'll throw them out.'

'I did my doings. Because of the journey.'

'That's good… I've two presents for you.'

'Presents?'

'This is from me. It's a book.'

'What book?'

'The one you wanted me to read to you.'

'Yes.'

'And this is from Mrs Capes. A bottle of scent.'

'How kind.'

'Will you write to me?'

'Letters?… Letters?'

'What else?'

'Yes, Susy. Yes.'

'I've written the address in the book. Nurse S. Barrow, The Jerusalem Home, and so on.'

'Thank you.'

*

Down one flight of steps, then another. Nurse Barrow carried the heavier case. A short corridor. Two more flights and they were passing the dining-hall. The ladies were at table. The creature wore her fur.

'She's asked Matron if she can have it buried with her,' said Nurse Barrow, immediately regretting the words. She looked at Mrs Gadny, who smiled.

Matron and Henry were waiting with two men in uniform by the bust of Lord Whatsit.

'Your son will travel with you.'

'Stepson.'

'In the ambulance.'

The men went out with the cases.

'Goodbye, Faith.'

'Goodbye, Matron.'

'Goodbye, Faith.'

'Goodbye, Susy.'

At the door Mrs Gadny said 'Do not spit, Matron' and laughed.

'On the wall,' Nurse Barrow explained.

'That wasn't me, Faith. That was a different matron.'

An ambulance driver ought to be more careful. He had a responsibility. She'd be falling off her perch at this rate.

'We're having a holiday, too. We've decided on the Costa

Brava. I should use the week for working but Thelma insists. Her mother will have the burden of the children.'

Henry was breathing loudly. She remembered how annoyed Tom was when he heard that Henry had been told by the army he wasn't healthy enough to train.

She had stared at the flowers on the walls and had searched her mind for things to say to him.

'Have you forgiven your father?'

'For what?'

'For beating you.'

It was years back, she knew, but – as Mrs Barber once said – some scars refused to heal.

'Yes, yes.' He was smiling as much as he could.

'Harry never forgave Barry.' The names confused her. 'Or was it the other way round? I do believe it was. Yes. It was Barry who never forgave.'

'Who are they?'

'I must tell you.'

She needed to talk to her stepson, she was pleased to find. Mrs Capes's stories would do the trick. They would keep his interest.

About the author

Paul Bailey was born in London in 1937. He won a scholar-ship to the Central School of Speech and Drama and worked as an actor from 1956 to 1964. He became a freelance writer in 1967.

He was appointed Literary Fellow at Newcastle and Durham Universities, and was Visiting Lecturer in English Literature at the North Dakota State University. He was awarded the E.M. Forster Award in 1974 and in 1978 he won the George Orwell Prize for his essay 'The Limitations of Despair'.

Paul Bailey has written eight novels, including *At the Jerusalem*, which won a Somerset Maugham Award and an Arts Council Writers' Award, and *Peter Smart's Confessions* and *Gabriel's Lament*, both of which were shortlisted for the Booker Prize. His non-fiction books include two volumes of memoir and a biography of three gay popular entertainers from the twentieth century.

He has also written plays for radio and television, and as a literary critic.

About the introducer

Colm Tóibín was born in Enniscorthy in 1955. He is the author of nine novels including *The Master, Brooklyn, The Testament of Mary* and *Nora Webster*. His work has been short-listed for the Booker Prize three times, has won the Costa Novel Award and the Impac Award. His most recent novel is *House of Names*. He has also published two collections of stories and many works of non-fiction. He lives in Dublin.